Ordinary Love & Good Will

ORDINARY LOVE & GOOD WILL

TWO NOVELLAS BY

Jane Smiley

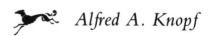 Alfred A. Knopf

NEW YORK   1989

THIS IS A BORZOI BOOK
PUBLISHED BY ALFRED A. KNOPF, INC.

Copyright © 1989 by Jane Smiley
All rights reserved under International
and Pan-American Copyright Conventions.
Published in the United States
by Alfred A. Knopf, Inc., New York,
and simultaneously in Canada by Random House
of Canada Limited, Toronto.
Distributed by Random House, Inc., New York.

Good Will was originally published in somewhat
different form in *Wigwag*.

Library of Congress Cataloging-in-Publication Data
Smiley, Jane.
   [Ordinary love]
   Ordinary love ; & Goodwill : two novellas / Jane Smiley.
      p.   cm.
   ISBN 0-394-57772-8
   I. Smiley, Jane.   Goodwill.   1989.   II. Title.
PS3569.M3907   1989
813'.54—dc20   89-45284
                                                          CIP

Manufactured in the United States of America
First Edition

ORDINARY
LOVE

I don't want Joe to find me on my knees, buffing the kitchen floor with an old cotton turtleneck, but he does, and says, "Mom! What are you doing? Relax!"

I sit back on my heels and say, "It's only six-thirty. What's with you?"

But I know. We both know. He crosses the kitchen and pours himself his first cup of coffee. He drinks them three at a time, I've noticed this summer, hot and with lots of milk and sugar. Now he turns away from the coffeemaker, and the cup is half empty before he sits at the table. He is grinning. Michael will be here today. Michael, Joe's identical twin, has been teaching mathematics in a secondary school in Benares, India for two years. That is why I am buffing the floor, why neither of us can relax.

The floor is pegged maple, about seventy-five years old. The boards vary in width from two inches to five, and are laid diagonally. In the last fifteen minutes, I have worked my way from the pantry to the back door, into a long bronze leaf of sunlight that colors my forearms and turns my hands muscular with shadows. I like this floor, troublesome as it is: caring for it, I remind myself of my mother, and this city, in spite of all its trees, seems rather like Nebraska, where I grew up. The long, rhythmic motions with the rag are soothing and productive at the same time.

Joe says, "I think I'll leave for the airport about nine." He is bouncing in his chair. I smile and say, "Why don't you leave now?"

"I'm relaxed, Mom. What makes you think I'm not re-laxed?" His expression is almost maniacal. They are twenty-five, and they have not seen each other in two years. "You, woman, get up and have a cup of tea or something." And so I do, simply for the pleasure of sitting at the kitchen table with my son. I let him make me toast and peel me an orange, and pour milk on my Rice Krispies. We talk about the geraniums in the window box and the broken lawnmower and the courses Joe is going to take when school starts again in two weeks. We don't talk about Michael. It is a family ritual, not to allude to the returning traveler while he or she is in transit. Usually we just don't speak the name, but this time Joe hasn't even said "he" or "my brother."

Joe has been with me all summer, the longest time we've spent together in six years, and I've gotten used to him. Joe was nervous about living with his mother all summer, but it has been one of the great summers of my life, the brush and thump and rattle of a congenial presence in the house every day. I'll be sorry when he goes back to school, and he knows it. He gets up from the table and goes into the dining room. He puts on some record, though only after carefully cleaning it off, and here comes Hank Williams, a compromise. I get back to the floor. He brought home his record collection and all summer his gift to me has been surprise music, but he can be pretty demanding—he's made me listen to Elvis Costello, The Talking Heads, The Flamin' Groovies, Dire Straits. I pretend I can hear the melodies. He says, only half joking, "This is pretty central to your mom-project, I would say, if you want to do it right." Doing it right involves learning to tolerate weirder harmonies than I was accustomed to before, but as a part of his "son-project" he plays the opera and the folk music I like.

He was living in Chicago, but his girlfriend broke up with him in June. After he got here, she wrote him four letters in two days, then that was it. Louise, her name is. She'd visited here four or five times, and I'd liked her, found her a pleasant, straightforward young woman. At lunch after he had been here a few days, he pushed one of the letters across the table for me to read. The important thing, she wrote, was that she didn't have the power to make him happy. Joe got up then and went to pull weeds in the flower beds. I remembered that feeling, life with a moody man, the ceiling lifting and lowering hour by hour, some days minute by minute. I thought she was wise to recognize her capacities before marriage, before children, but when Joe passed the kitchen window, I saw from the angle of his shoulders that he was devastated, and tears came into my eyes for him. Since then he hasn't dated.

His whole social life here revolves around Barbara and Kevin, friends from high school who got married at the end of college. When they come over, she always wants to sit me in the kitchen and talk about furniture and he always wants to take me outside (No eavesdroppers? I wonder) and probe my knowledge of state government. I am fifty-two years old, which turns out to be the age when your children and their friends are suddenly eager to plunder the knowledge and experience they once wouldn't admit you had for nuggets they now find useful. I am an accountant for the state, in the DOT, which must explain Kevin's interest.

I've been married once, almost married a second time. I have five children, four grandchildren, which must explain Barbara's interest, even though furniture is the closest she can get to the real topic of children and family life. My younger daughter, Annie, who had a baby in May, calls about everything now, though for years I hardly heard from her. My elder daughter, Ellen, lives a mile from here. She has two daughters of her own, and she talks to me or stops by every day. Daniel, a year younger than Ellen, lives in New York. He has one son, and calls every weekend. Once I was the font of wisdom about babies that they think I am now. My hip was made for carrying an infant; I could thread my way among toys and toddlers without stumbling, hardly looking down, except to admire a scribbled drawing. I thought four high chairs at the kitchen table and two big Labrador retrievers milling around them hoovering up the jetsam was unremarkable.

After buffing the floor, I go into the bathroom and scour the tub and the sink. I love this house. I used to drive past it every day on my way to work, and then it came up for sale, and I bought it. It is a four-bedroom Colonial Revival, on a huge corner lot, with a wraparound porch downstairs and a second-story walk-out balcony, too much for a single woman, but just enough, in a way, for me. I think of it as my acreage. Here alone, the way I usually am, I appreciate the largeness of its peace—no grandeur, but plenty of roomy quiet. There are three chestnut trees in the yard that must be indestructible, since there aren't three chestnuts so close together anywhere else in the state. By the time I have done the bathroom and straightened the living room, it is nearly nine. Joe is whistling through the house, making himself, I know, wait until the exact minute before letting himself depart. I stand in the shadow of the living room doorway, and soon enough he comes downstairs, putting his things into his pockets, jaunty with anticipation. I admire him. He is tall and square-shouldered. He stands up straight. He is slender, with large hands and feet, and though he doesn't have the air of physical know-how that, say, Daniel has, he has repaired a lot of things around the house this summer, and cut a lot of wood with the chain saw he bought when

he got here. The man he is going to the airport to get now
is his exact copy, top to toe, hair, fingers, feet. I haven't
seen them together in years. He shouts, "I'm going now,
okay?" I say, softly, "Okay," and he turns. He exclaims,
"No big deal, Mom!"

"Oh, yeah. Right. I remember. Who cares?"

Just after he leaves, the phone rings, and it is Ellen. She
says, "What time did you say he's getting here?"

"Joe just left. I'd say they'll be back before noon."

"Can I come over?"

"Of course."

"We knew this guy in Philadelphia who came back from
India after two years. He was very weird."

"How was he weird?"

"Well, he would pick up the napkin you'd given him at
dinner and he would say, 'This cloth is big enough to make
a whole garment for an Indian child.' He would say that
sort of thing all the time. I worry that Joe doesn't know
what to expect."

"They've written a lot."

"Letters are very deceptive, I think."

"Well, I, for one, can't wait to see him." I am tempted
to say his name, but at the last second I don't dare.

"I hate this," she says. Then, "Are you coming here
tomorrow night?"

"What time do you want us?"

"Six. I don't think I'll come over there today after all.
Jerry's out and I have too many errands."

"That's fine." I wait a long moment for her to decide to
hang up the phone.

As I turn toward the kitchen, an ancient wave of terror
seems to unroll from my head downward. I know exactly
where it comes from. When Ellen was ten and the twins
were five, and there were two in between, Pat, their father,
and I parted, and he sold our house without telling me and

took the children abroad. The morning I saw them for the first time in almost a year, this terror was so strong that I staggered from one side of the walk to the other as I approached his new house. I knew they were watching from the windows, and I was trying with all my concentration to walk normally, but I was literally unbalanced by the prospect of seeing them. There are things we can do in our family—eat peacefully, lend money, confide—but reunions are fraught with echoes.

When Michael walks into the house, he is not Joe's twin, but a shadow of Joe, dressed all in white cotton and cadaverous. He greets me in a Michael-like way, "Hey, Ma! I'm back. Any calls?"—grinning, grabbing me around the waist, and kissing me on the lips, but his biceps are like strings, and his ribs press into me through his shirt. It is all I can do not to recoil in surprise. We try to maintain a light, ironic (though sometimes rueful) atmosphere around here, but I look at Joe, and see by his subdued smile that Michael's figure has pierced him, too. He sets down the bags. In the moment we wait for Michael to signal us what to do and how to act, I think an irresistible thought—that we have gotten back less than we sent out.

Michael says, "You changed the pictures."

My glance follows his, and I realize that some copies I'd had of Audubon birds are missing. Joe says, "I moved the sunflower pictures down here from the guest room. Mom didn't even notice. I did it at the end of June."

"Of course I noticed." The sunflower pictures are rather nice: all five children and myself picnicking in a field of wild sunflowers on my mother's farm in Nebraska. The twins had just learned how to walk. My mother, too, ill but happy. She is sitting in a lawn chair, a profusion of sunflowers laced around her, on the only hummock for miles in any direction. I didn't notice he moved them because this is where they used to hang, before I decided that I wanted to give the house a more decorative, impersonal look. The fact is, he's also shifted the furniture in the living room and the guest bedroom, and when he makes dinner, he always serves it on the oldest plates. All summer he has been quizzing me about our history, especially his early childhood with Michael in our old house. I don't object, but I always think, At least Michael wants to grow up and get on with his life. And he does: he looks at the pictures with only minimal interest, then goes into the dining room and puts his shoulder bag on the table. His glance around is appreciative but not lingering. From the back, he looks more like himself. His shoulders have lost none of their breadth, and he moves supplely still. I say, "Darling, are you tired? or hungry?"

He turns and smiles merrily. "Don't I look hungry?"

"Well—"

"Ma! Open your eyes! I'm starving!"

In a sense, we find out over lunch, this is literally true. Joe serves up yogurt with wheat germ and raisins, peanut-butter sandwiches, a piece of Brie cheese, fresh peaches. Michael stirs his yogurt and says in a jolly tone, "My intestines are unrecognizable. I mean, my large intestine is like a piece of PVC pipe, and it all just shoots through. That's what happens to everybody." He lifts up his cloth napkin, but doesn't say anything about how many children it could clothe.

Joe says, "What happens to everybody?"

"Oh. Amebic dysentery. I've had it for over a year. I need to get some Bactrim. Or I could get cured. You can do that here."

"Can't you get cured there?"

"You keep getting reinfected, so it isn't worth it."

"Attractive," says Joe.

"Oh, I ran around like crazy when I first realized I had it, looking for a doctor who would make it go away, or at least be IMPRESSED. Now I hardly think about it."

"You could find a job as a pencil." They laugh.

In the middle of a peach, he puts his head in his hand and rests his elbow on the table. I say, "Tired?"

"Turned around. Jet-lagged. Twenty-four hours in transit is no joke. And they always make you leave in the middle of the night, and the night before, you were out with your friends. I'm glad I went west, though. They say it takes weeks to recover from flying through Hawaii. This stewardess on the flight was telling me that she hasn't had her period in a year, because she flies New York–New Delhi. North-south, they're regular as clockwork, but these east-west ones wonder if they'll ever be able to get pregnant." He clears his throat, and I realize that this is a new habit he has. It reminds me of my farmer uncles.

If I was waiting for tales of the exotic, and I think I was, I guess I am to be disappointed. I make one try: "Do you miss it? Did you like it?"

He looks at me thoughtfully. He says, "I got used to it." That's all.

Joe and I exchange covert smiles every so often, smiles of relief. Sometime during lunch Michael himself seems to have reappeared, swimming up through the strangeness of his clothing and his talk and his emaciation, a Michael familiar enough to recognize and love.

Once, on a trip to Washington, D.C., I saw a childhood friend in line next to me in a deli. I hadn't seen her since we were both in fifth grade, eating lunch together beside the swing set in the school yard. I recognized her by a vein that ran up the center of her forehead to a slight widow's peak. She wasn't looking toward me, so I didn't speak for a minute, and in that minute this same thing happened, the ten-year-old face I perfectly remembered blossomed on the surface of this unknown, rather careworn woman. Before I even remembered her name, I was filled with a thirty-year-old fondness for how familiar and changeless she was. It's tempting to believe this is going to be simple.

I am planning a picnic for this evening, out in Eagle Point Park, but I have saved the shopping. Joe stands behind me, doing the dishes. Michael is upstairs. Joe says, "Coffee filters. And ice cream. Garbage bags." I write it down. "Alfalfa sprouts. Some of their marinated tofu." Joe says, "I wish it were next week. I wish I could ignore him."

"Do you think he'd like acidophilus milk?"

"I wish I could say, 'Hey, great to have you back, catch ya later, okay?' "

I get up casually, and go into the pantry and look at the shelves. Joe raises his voice: "I saw this coming. I almost got a ticket to the Bruce Springsteen concert. For tonight. In Detroit. I had my checkbook out, and the guy said a hundred and fifty. I said, 'How about two hundred?' I wanted to be sure I'd go, you know."

I don't respond, and he turns off the water. "I knew I wouldn't. I knew I'd sit around here listening to him breathe."

The grocery store is my favorite place, a kind of meditation center that always refreshes me, but today it isn't enough. I'm still reluctant to go home when I pull out of the parking lot, and my reluctance grows as I near my house. The easiest thing, like stepping off a high diving board, is to roll right past it and discover myself ten minutes later at another mall, melting ice cream and acidophilus milk notwithstanding.

The mirrors behind window displays reveal me, and for a while I stand staring at myself without realizing what I am looking at. In fact, an anniversary is passing this weekend—it is twenty years since Pat and I parted. If my children notice, they will undoubtedly not mention it. I won't mention it, either, though this time of year often makes me think of that life.

I loved having twins, even though there were three children under five years old already running around the place. We lived in a huge old house on five acres of ground. My favorite moment of the day was in the morning, when I would be lying in bed, nursing the twins, one on each side, and then the other children would come and climb under the covers, and the dogs, too. I would be buried in flesh and noise, all thoughts scattered. We were twenty-seven, and drunk with the immensity of the world we had already made.

Pat's pediatric-allergy research was celebrated. Work he did led to the discovery that the newborn's stomach wall is a semipermeable membrane, and that nonhuman milk can cross undigested into the child's body and set up an allergic reaction. But his great hero was Piaget. He loved the idea that a child's brain development was orderly, a natural perpetual-motion machine that only had to be set going once. If anyone objected to this image as too mechanistic, he would say, "The mind is a palpable thing, as physical as anything else. It doesn't create order, it IS order. It also FEELS order. Order feels good. Thinking feels good. Mmmm." (He'd rub his hands over his head, the children would laugh.) "Brains are in no danger of getting mechanical, but someday machines are going to be fleshy." He also loved the idea of researching his own children, but he recognized that even Piaget's sample would be considered laughably small these days. In the *Guinness Book of World Records*, there was a Russian woman who had sixty-nine children. This didn't seem impossible to Pat.

No matter how busy he was, Pat insisted on a nightly family dinner, and he was sparkling at the table. No matter how young the children were, he addressed them with arresting hypotheses, pointed questions, opinions about their opinions. He was wooing them. He wooed me the same way. And, really, it was hard to take your eyes from his face, whether you were his child or his wife.

Well, in the midst of all of this, I fell in love with a man in our neighborhood. Pat sold the house and took the children to England, and my life was utterly formless, nothing, so close to nonbeing that I was surprised to find my clothes in the closet every morning. When I remember that time, twenty years ago now, the light around me seems to have been blinding. Shades could not be drawn against it. I seem to be walking down a city sidewalk and lost in the glare. I seem always to be waking up in the middle of the night, terrified to find all the lights on in my extraordinary new apartment. There is no known cause that speaks to what that time seemed like to me. It cannot be understood, really, only re-experienced unexpectedly. That sometimes happens to me.

Pat stopped doing allergy research twelve years ago, after the axle on his van broke near Winter Park, Colorado, and the van rolled over the side of the road and down into the valley. No fire, thank God. Annie, Michael, Tatty (Pat's second wife), their two children (Sara, Kenny), and Daniel were sprayed over the mountainside like a handful of gravel. Michael, Tatty, and Daniel got up and walked away. Annie broke her leg, Sara broke some ribs and her pelvis, Kenny and Pat were knocked unconscious. The little boy came to about three days later, but Pat was out for three and a half weeks, and when he came to, thinking didn't feel so good anymore—neither as sensuous nor as effective as before. His doctors didn't see how he was even going to practice medicine again, much less do research, but they underestimated his will, as I had once but wouldn't have again. The accident was a boon to me, though, because he relaxed completely about the custody arrangements. In fact, the first time in six years that Joe and Michael spent more than a few weeks together was when Michael lived with me while Pat was in physical therapy.

When I tell Joe about the old days, I emphasize what he wants to hear about, their pleasures, hoping he will ask the natural question, why did I leave? But the dazzling family photo invites contemplation and repels inquiry. When the children were younger, not having to explain was a relief, but now it annoys me that they don't ask, that they are interested only in what they can remember, as if it hadn't ever occurred to them that their father and I had inner lives.

When Pat and I first met, in college, we often studied together. I would be sitting across from him in the library, and I would look up from my book and say, "Here's something."

"What?" he would say, practically snapping to attention. What I had thought to be of passing interest would now take on profound fascination as I read it aloud, and Pat would inhale it. A few hours or a few days later, he would give it back, in talk or as gifts—books, records, tickets to a performance.

I would like to tell Joe what a peculiar and suffocating feeling it got to be, to be attended to so closely, to have every idle remark sucked up and transformed into a theory, to be made relentlessly significant, oneself and an enlarged model of oneself, the Visible Woman, always being told what she was like and what it meant.

When I get home, Joe is sitting at the kitchen table, reading the autobiography of Bertrand Russell. His field is the history of science. He is specializing in medieval technological innovations, but his private obsession is stupidity—lots of the greatest mathematicians and physicists have been slow-speaking, slow-thinking. "People," Joe says, "who come to a boulder in the road and stop and scratch their heads and finally sit down next to the boulder and contemplate it for a long time. No one who is really stupid would ever consider just walking around it and continuing down the road." A sign of genius, Joe thinks. He has a challenging, rather crude way of phrasing these ideas, as if they have met opposition, even if I don't disagree. I set the bags on the counter, and he says, "Taking a nap."

"Well, I'm sure he needs one."

He closes the book. "I'm not getting through this very fast. I was intending to have it read by this morning."

"Maybe we should send him back to India. I found the abundance at the grocery store awfully embarrassing." We look at each other and smile. Joe has a pleasant face. Most mothers of identical twins assert that they have never mistaken one for the other. I assert it, too. But, inevitably, one twin is the theme and one is the variation. Michael was "aggressive," "cheery," "sturdy," "harum-scarum." Michael was himself. Joe, second-born, was nearly a pound lighter than Michael at birth, and Joe was somehow always more or less—even when Michael wasn't around, Joe was "more frustrated," "quieter," "thinner," "more studious," "better organized." The comparative belonged to Joe even if the terms weren't at all the same. Then, when Joe was living with me and Michael with Pat, it was Joe who talked of himself this way, as if continual comparison and contrast would call up Michael's ghostly presence. After this summer, though, I am so used to Joe and we have talked about so many things that I've forgotten, every so often, about Michael. I am sure this is a good sign, a sign that maybe Joe, too, has let him go a time or two. Now I say, and even as I say it I recognize and enjoy the intimacy of it, "Do you think you're afraid of having him back? Of the closeness, I mean?"

He turns the book over once, looking at it rather than at me. "No. I was afraid he would go away as my twin and come back as my brother. I don't want that." He sighs. "He doesn't either."

"I'm sure he doesn't."

"There are a lot of things that are unspoken between us, you know."

"That's always been true." I sit at the table, groping for the most delicate kind of tact. This is an argument we have been tending toward all summer, and I don't want to have it now. "I think it's important that we don't seem clinging. He went far away. He must have known he would come back different from you as well as from his old self. Maybe he intended it."

"I think he thought it was a price he might have to pay for getting away from everything else." He says this in a detached but definite tone, as if he isn't going to listen to any more on the subject. We smile again, a truce, and he says, "I might have fixed the lawnmower." He puts his hand in his pocket. "There are just these few leftover items." He pulls out two screws of different sizes, a washer, and a bolt that will fit neither screw. "Think they're important, or can we ignore them?" I laugh, then Joe laughs. I say, "I think you'd better go back and try again. But the leftover parts are getting smaller, at least."

"Just promise me you won't sneak it out of the garage and over to the repair shop."

"Not on a bet. I want to see you rise to the challenge."

"Haven't thrown anything yet. Only rammed my head into the wall of the garage once."

Now there is a shout from the living room, and Ellen appears, framed by the living room doorway, but standing back, suspicious. Joe pushes his chair back and says, "He's asleep." Relieved, Ellen steps into the kitchen. She doesn't speak. She never does, right at first. She picks up Joe's book and looks at it, then turns and looks into one of the cupboards by the sink. She takes out a glass and runs herself a drink of water. "Well?" she says.

"Thin," I say. "Amebic dysentery."

"Ugh. Right in the house here, huh?"

"It's not like that," snaps Joe.

"I was only making a joke."

"Not funny." They look at each other. He is glaring. She is considering. I say, "I thought you weren't coming over."

She throws up her hands.

I can hear Tracy and Diane in the front yard. Joe put up a tire swing for them in June, and they have been all over it, having fun, I say. "Building poignant memories," Joe says. His nostalgia is militant, almost hard, almost a reproach.

"So how are you?" says Ellen to Joe, and he stops glaring. He says, "I don't know." Then he says, annoyed, "What's the big deal? I mean, he went away and he came back. He told us he was going away, and how long he was going to be gone, and he came back when he said he would. I'm pissed off."

"At whom?" says Ellen.

"At myself, of course," says Joe. And he goes over to the coffeemaker and pours himself a cup of coffee and drinks it down. Then he slams out the back door, saying, "I'm going to start over on the lawnmower now."

Ellen says, "Is he still fixing the lawnmower?"

"Fixing it again."

"Would you just borrow ours and cut the grass? The police are going to cite you pretty soon."

"Let them." But before I've even finished speaking, she has picked up Joe's book and started reading it. She can't resist. She even says, "Hmm!" in a surprised and interested voice. I know the rudeness she treats me with is a habit, but is calculated, too, as a test of how much familiarity I will allow. Our conversation must always seem as if it has no breaks, is uninterrupted by formal greetings or farewells, is beyond routine civilities, is as close to mind-reading as possible.

Now Ellen puts the book down and looks at me expectantly. I say, "Smooth enough so far."

"Curiosity got the better of me. I can't wait to see him. Are you sure he's asleep?"

"No. Actually, he's probably hiding out like the rest of us. I'd like to let him come back in his own time. What's Jerry doing today?"

"Soloing, can you believe it?" She makes a face. Jerry has been taking flying lessons. "I was trying to forget about it. This morning I sent the girls up to wake him. I sent them up in their underpants, so he could see their defenseless little bodies and have some second thoughts. But all he did was get them all excited about when they can go flying with Daddy." She eyes me, then goes to the doorway, where she can see the girls. "Speaking of daddies, Daddy sent me a check for five hundred dollars. The network had the news to him about our car being vandalized within twenty-four hours. Does he think we don't have insurance or something?"

"I don't know what he thinks."

She spins toward me. "He thinks that just because Jerry owns a bookstore we can't afford those little amenities like collision insurance."

"Send it back."

"Then he would call up and want to talk about it. He watches his bank statement, too. If you don't cash the check right away, he thinks you're resisting."

"Aren't you?"

"Of course."

"Does he know Michael is coming home this weekend?"

"I'm sure the network phoned him the moment the plane

touched down. Now he's counting the minutes until he gets his call. It would be almost easier to have him living in town." The way Pat seems always to know what's going on with his children is, admittedly, uncanny. The children used to call him "the fourth man," after Daniel read some books about Kim Philby. When Anthony Blunt revealed himself, Pat became "the controversial fifth man," and Joe and Ellen still sometimes refer to him as "Five."

"Anyway, I hate him having insights into me."

I shrug. Ellen and I have talked about this, a little, but she, too, seems to drift away when I begin to allude to my life with her father. She always interrupts with a question about how I managed to get five children into snowsuits, or were there really three potty chairs in a row in the downstairs bathroom.

"Especially since they aren't matched by any into himself " She goes into the living room and calls out the front door after Tracy and Diane. I open the dishwasher and put some cups into it. Maybe because Michael has returned, it suddenly seems rich and luxurious to have Ellen and Joe and the girls around, a mother's feeling that I resented when my mother thought it of me, her only child. Those days I thought nothing would stop me from going to Alaska. Or Singapore. Or New Zealand. That, even if I were to have children when I grew up, they wouldn't really notice my absence. Unlike a daughter, a mother might slip away without saying when she would be back. But Ellen and Joe are as exacting in this regard as any parent. Ellen won't even let me leave my car at the airport. She insists on seeing me off and meeting my plane, and Joe always has me send him a copy of my itinerary. For a long time, the first thing I did when I arrived at any hotel was ask for my mail, knowing that there would be a postcard waiting from Joe, saying something like, "Dear Mom, Here you are, sitting right across the table. You just gave me my orange-juice-egg-

and-brewer's-yeast breakfast. Now I am about to shock you by drinking it. Well, Mom, I just wanted to say hi, and enjoy your trip." Annie and Daniel are less attentive, but they keep tabs, all the same. From all of this I know that their father must have told them I left them, and that this became knowledge for them that transcended information. When I've asked what their father did tell them, they can't remember. "Something good, I'm sure," says Joe. "Dad's never at a loss for a theory." From their point of view, I deserved this reputation of being ready for anything, untrustworthy, liable to slip the traces. I suppose this is my penance—always to be reminded by their care that I got away from them once.

I am not the first to vanish, though they don't know it. My mother had a cousin. She'd be over a hundred now, but when I was about ten and she was sixty, and I suppose everyone thought her emotional life had run its course, she fled to Denver. All of the men in the family went after her, four farmers in overalls leaving their land in the middle of the summer and, what was more shocking, spending money on the train fare. She was married to her second cousin, Uncle Karl, who was prosperous and sober, and didn't beat her, so it was obvious to everyone that she must be insane for leaving him. They brought her back and put her in a state mental hospital. My father and uncles were kindly men, and got her out of the asylum after about a year. She stayed home, cured, and died in her nineties. I never talked to her about it. In fact, I hardly ever talked to her throughout my teens, because I didn't want the men to make the criminal connection that I thought was there. But I know one thing about her. She was never left alone again. One relative or another was always assigned to her, for her own good.

I was born in 1934, into an extended family that was so hardworking and so closely knit that they survived the Depression with their farms intact, paid for, and, in some cases, improved. Scandinavian tenacity, Scandinavian silence. Pat, whose background was Chicago Irish, had a lot of insights into my family, too. Because of us, he got interested in genetics, and did an important comparative longitudinal study of recurring allergic reactions among Irish families in Chicago and Norwegian families in northwestern Iowa. He also read all the major Icelandic sagas, and conceived a fondness for Knut Hamsun and Sigrid Undset.

Everyone called him a genius, though Joe would say that he was too quick for that. Joe is a little dismissive of Pat's "brilliance." Joe has worked out a system, a rainbow of intelligence that runs from stupid, obvious red to subtle, mysterious violet. He envies Pat's "brilliance" (a pure, direct blue) from the vantage point of his own just-above-average green ("bright"), and although I discourage his envy and find these rankings absurd, secretly I know better than Joe does that once there was something to envy, in those years when Pat was discovering his powers.

Though he practices medicine still, I suspect that Pat never really recovered from the accident, and of all the lost things, maybe Pat's intelligence is the most unusual. It might have been genius, the spectrum bending, red meeting violet one impossible time. To me, it was more like a vocal timbre, movingly distinct, undefinable, fleeting. Ellen did spectacularly in school, but really none of the children have just what Pat had. It could have something to do with how inbred his Irish relatives in Chicago were—his aunts still spoke with a brogue, though two generations removed from Ireland. When he married me, Norwegian got in, another pure strain, but dogged, never scintillating, always cautious yellow, Joe would say, yellow the color of sunflowers and late-summer fields.

"Where would it get you?" I say. "Where has it gotten him?" Joe knows better than to allude to Pat's accomplishments as a researcher, which are nice, but not the point, or even to his accomplishments as a diagnostician, which are nicer, because more humane, but still not the point. He always shrugs. Pat is not happy, not at peace, not possessed of much self-knowledge, not even rich, for a specialist. He has what he could have had with only average intelligence —two wives, nine children, a sense that there is something missing. Well, I have another image of the mind, any mind, no special mind. It is a wheel, like a paddlewheel, turning slowly, with a kind of ordered vastness, bigger than it seems to be, going deeper, and bringing up more unrecognizable wealth than anyone thought possible. Brilliance is like little round red reflectors nailed to the crosspieces, eye-catching, lovely, in certain lights dazzling, but little even so, pure decoration. Joe doesn't listen to me. He has spent his whole life in school, where brilliance is prized, and anyway, I am only his mom.

Behind me, the screen door slams. Joe comes in, dripping with sweat, and followed by Tracy, who is carrying the Crescent wrench. I can see Diane through the screen, watching him. They are eight and six, his girls. He is patient with his nieces as he never is with himself, and they have been helping him, in a manner of speaking, with the lawnmower project. If one of them makes a suggestion, he will take the time to try it out, rather than declaring that it couldn't possibly work. In return, they worry about him. Diane leaves him notes with coins folded into them, because she can see that he doesn't have a job.

"Tracy and Diane want to come with me to the hardware store. I need to find something to loosen the flywheel."

Ellen comes in from the living room. "Which one are you going to? That one by the liquor store?"

"That one is fine." And so they all go out together, companionable, Ellen and Joe bumping into one another, Diane slipping her hand into her mother's hand and Ellen squeez-

another cup of coffee. A few minutes later, Michael comes in, dressed in jeans and a shirt, barefoot. "Hi, Mom," he says, warmly.

"Sleep?" I say.

"Pretty good, for a mere eight hours." He sets a large round pink object on the table beside his plate. Joe looks at it, too. We exchange a glance. Michael runs himself a glass of water, then sits down and puts this pink object in his mouth. With some water and a visible gulp, he swallows it. Joe says, "Good Lord, what's that?" I put the cakes in the oven.

"Chloroquine. Quinine. Malaria, you know."

"You have malaria?"

"Maybe. At any rate, I have to take this pill every Sunday. 'Instead of church'—that's what the Indian doctors always say."

"What are you taking for the tuberculosis?"

"Tuberculosis?"

"All that coughing and throat-clearing in the bathroom."

"Oh. What? Oh, that. That's just a habit. India is so dusty that your throat gets hypersensitive to phlegm. It goes away, I hear. Hey, Joe. Don't worry about me, all right?"

"How about this. I won't talk about it."

"Mom can worry about me. She owes me for all those letters she didn't write. Shit, I am so jet-lagged."

"You should have said something before we went out last night."

"Why?"

"You didn't seem to have a good time."

"I didn't have a good time, but I had a good enough time. I'm glad we went out. Barbara and Kevin seem happy with each other."

"It was a nice wedding," I say.

"I would like that, I think," says Michael, "being married to somebody I'd known since seventh grade. Or maybe

"Stanley!"

"Yes, Ollie?"

"Pull the fucking cord!"

We laugh. Michael pulls the cord. Noise bursts out of the lawnmower, and Michael gestures toward the handle, shouting, "After you, Oliver!"

At lunch they are still at it, though by now Michael is the Lone Ranger and Joe is Tonto. I remember this particular dialogue, because they developed it years ago. They switch off roles, and sometimes one of them is Silver, the horse. When they were fourteen and both living with me, they went for two weeks with Michael as Tonto and Joe as Silver, arguing about whether the Lone Ranger was primarily racist or primarily "human-ist." I put bowls of soup in front of them, and Michael says, in a deep, pompous voice, "Fine soup, ma'am. Back in that box canyon up Cheyenne way, we were reduced to eating our shoes."

"Shoe taste good to red man."

"Tonto here caught some lizards for our delectation, though."

Joe makes a face at me behind his hand. "Lizard taste good to white man. Red man not like tickle going down."

"What was that, faithful sidekick?"

"Was, 'fuck you,' Kemosabe."

"Why, certainly, my good man."

It occurs to me that, with enough repairs, comic routines, and information about sports and music, Michael and Joe might come together in peace.

Joe gets up for another cup of coffee, and starts rummaging in the refrigerator. In this interim Michael puts down his fork and rubs his face in his hands, yawning. It is easy to forget what he has to recover from. I have already gotten used to his appearance, and other new habits —waggling his head when he means to nod "yes" and stooping because he has spent so much time talking to short

kind of project they write about in magazines, where someone buys a place with no floors, missing walls, no banisters, a hole where the toilet should be, a laundry sink as the only appliance in the kitchen. I think that inside that house he was utterly happy, because he was surrounded by his project. And he didn't throw himself into it, either. It took him a year to get the floor down between the basement and the first floor. He was a patient man. I don't know that my children ever really liked him. He must have seemed much duller to them than their father. He wasn't talkative and didn't smile very often, although, when he did, I found his smile merry and disarming. He didn't read much, didn't talk about the nature of anything—the brain, life, the ways of the world. And he was moody, too. Simon was the kind of man who would have been a good husband in the eyes of my father and uncles—good job, practical intelligence—and in the eyes of my mother and aunts—keeps out of the way, gives the wife a fairly free hand. Well, I might have married him, but he never thought he deserved me enough to ask. And I let the moment pass.

At eleven-thirty, when I am moving on to the editorial section of the Sunday paper, dreading a little the mishmash of misinformation and strong opinion that I will find there about the Naval Weapons Support Center, Joe comes in and says, "Hey, guess what's left this time!" He holds out his hand, closed.

"What?"

He opens his hand. "Nothing! And we didn't lose anything, either. Come on out."

The sun is hot already, and my sneakers stick a little to the asphalt of the driveway. Michael is filling the tank with gasoline. He stands back, puts down the can, hands the pull cord to Joe, saying, "After you, Oliver."

"Be my guest, Stanley."

"Age before beauty, Ollie."

falling in love with someone in seventh grade, and then having her grow up pretty, and shorter than me, and smart, and funny, too. You'd never have to fall in love again. In India you don't have to fall in love at all." Two bowls of shredded wheat, a hard-boiled egg, two pieces of toast, a glass of orange juice. He pushes himself away from the table. "Show me the lawnmower." Joe follows him out.

I suppose it is still my privilege to rummage in their rooms for dirty clothes, but I must say that I pause before doing it. Joe has left some shirts and underwear by the door of his room, and I pick up those, but when I go into Michael's room, I don't know where to begin. The bags he has brought—a knapsack and a duffel—have been emptied on the carpeting, a swath of unfamiliar, filmy items, all crumpled. There is a small pile of what look like tiny cigars, each tied with a red thread. There are pairs of sandals, some colorful pictures on parchmentlike paper, some books, a pile of blue air letters. The visible ones carry Joe's handwriting. I go to the window and open it, intending to ask what I can wash, and I see them in the driveway in front of the garage, squatting over the lawnmower. The tools are arranged in a neat row behind them. As I watch, Joe lifts out the motor and they turn. Joe puts it down on a piece of newspaper, and they stare at it for a long time. Finally, Michael points at something, and a moment later, Joe chooses a tool and applies it to the motor. After that, it is beguiling to watch how they cooperate, with nods and exchanged glances and passing of tools and laughter. I turn and leave Michael's room, stepping over the clothes.

Simon Elliott was like that, handy with tools. This house is full of his work—new wiring, new chimney, floors refinished, new shower upstairs, bookshelves built into the dining-room walls. I didn't let him do as much as he wanted to—barnboard siding in the basement, tiling around the fireplace, downstairs bathroom. His own house was the

tofu and avocado, tomato slices, sprouts, sliced chicken breast, a loaf of bread. Finally, he says, "Mom! Sit down."

"We don't want to start too late. It takes a while to get there, and it isn't light all that long this time of year. I like to have time for a little walk along the creek." I rummage for the Swiss cheese.

"Hey, Mom. You're avoiding me." Joe would have made it a question. I look at him, startled, and there is Joe's smile, warm, familiar, almost conspiratorial. It is uncanny, but I sit down. After a moment, I look Michael square in the face, and his gaze is steady on mine. It is a handsome face, more masculine than when he left. The nose and chin have taken their adult size. They have the prominence that Pat's nose and chin had. His lips are no longer as full as they were ten years ago, but they have more softness than men's lips usually have. His eyes are thickly lashed and an almost tawny brown. There is hair curling out of the loose collar of his shirt where there didn't use to be. Well, he is a man now. I see that his hair is like mine, straight and thick, plain brown. I look and look, as if looking at an object, and he lets me. His eyes are affectionate and receptive, and I also look at the outline of my head reflected in their pupils. He says, "Hi, Mom."

"Hi, Michael."

"What are you thinking, Mom?"

"I'm thinking that all your glands are fully operational now. I bet you've even had sex with a girl or two."

This is something I've done all summer with Joe, refer to subjects usually taboo between mother and son. I would like my sons to make of me what I am, just an adult woman, but an adult woman in every way. I would like them to do me that favor, now, before they have wives. He says, "What's a girl?" Then, "You didn't write me very much, Mom."

"Once a month."

ing it without hesitating in what she is saying to Joe. Their coming seems to have soothed him a bit.

As Joe's car turns into the street, Michael comes down the back stairs and says, "Hey, Mom."

"Hi, sweetheart. Did you sleep?"

"Kind of. I knew where I was the whole time, though. Any coffee made?" He stretches, sits at the table, rubs his face in both his palms. "I called Annie and Daniel. I couldn't resist that phone where you just push a button and it dials the number for you. I just said hi, though."

"You can talk more later. They're coming for Labor Day weekend, anyway." I am shocked anew by the way his thighs spread to nothing against the seat of his chair, by the hollow of his stomach. The loose cotton of his clothing folds freely against his body, as substantial as he is. I set a cup of coffee in front of him, and he reaches for the cream and sugar. Half the cup vanishes in the first gulp. I am familiar with the twin studies that show similar attitudes, mannerisms, and life patterns in separated identical twins, but it is disconcerting all the same. He sits up straight, shoulders down, only his head bent, just like Joe does. He turns and smiles at me when he catches me looking at him, and his smile is first closed, then open, like Joe's. More than that, it communicates the same warmth and familiarity that I have seen in Joe's smile all summer, and attributed to all the time we have spent together. "Hungry?" I say.

"Always."

"Anything you can't eat?"

"I haven't eaten much meat in the last two years. Right now, you know what I would like?"

"No."

"A big bowl of chocolate ice cream."

I oblige him.

While he eats, I arrange things for the picnic—marinated

He says, "Ma, that was very strange of you to pull my hair."

"It struck me as the thing to do. My mother always used to do that to me." We smile. Michael's tongue comes out to lick the tears off his lips. I say, "Go wash your face in cold water."

He goes up the stairs. When the others come in, Ellen goes straight to the phone and hits the button that automatically dials her number. The first thing she says is, "Are you still alive?" Then she laughs in relief, and says, "Don't tell me a thing about it. If the wings wiggled on the landing or something, you have to keep it to yourself, okay?" A pause. "Seven landings? Oh, Lord, Jerry." I take the girls into the living room. While Ellen is talking and I am listening, I am also admiring the Frisbee and the yoyos Joe bought them at the hardware store. It surprises me to discover that I am as relieved as Ellen that Jerry has survived his solo flight. Jerry, I have to say, has persisted in these flying lessons in the face of Ellen's determined opposition. He is not much younger than I am—forty-six, I think. Like me, he has lived more than one life. He was a social worker in Cleveland for a long time. He got a master's in public policy as a last-ditch effort to save his interest in his career, and that was when he met Ellen, who was taking a course he was assisting in. She is slightly built, with porcelain skin and full lips, so I can imagine how malleable, or even delicate, he thought she was. When she first brought him home, he turned to me once and said, fondly, "She talks tough, doesn't she?" Now she sometimes remarks that, if Jerry had listened to what she said when she was a nineteen-year-old undergraduate and he was her thirty-five-year-old instructor, he wouldn't be so surprised at what he's gotten himself into. The two of them do pretty well with the bookstore, and he does a little consulting on the side. Since he is so near to me in age, one feeling I have about him is that he

isn't my type. His anxieties are displayed on the surface, and he is very talkative. I am glad Ellen is with him, though, because she is what my mother always called "a tartar" and he's good at short-circuiting her passions before they really take hold. She hangs up and comes into the living room. "So where is he?" she says. "I came over here three hours ago, and I still haven't seen the man of the hour."

Joe, who is sitting on the piano bench, tying a knot in one of the yoyo strings, says, "Doesn't he get back next week sometime? What's his name again?"

"Actually, that guy we knew made people call him 'Ravi' after he came back from India, and then he took a vow of silence for three months. He was going to build this geodesic dome that Jerry was supposed to go in on with him, but he only got as far as the scale model, which he glued together out of Ohio Blue Tip matches. He would hold it over his head and look through it and say, 'This is a much more human space.' "

"These things do not come solely from traveling to India." Joe rolls up the yoyo and tries it out, making it sleep at the bottom for ten or fifteen seconds; then he hands it to Tracy.

"I guess we'll see, won't we?" says Ellen. She speaks cheerfully, but it's clear she's needling him. "After that, he took seventy-five psilocybin trips—"

"Would you shut up?"

"This was fifteen years ago, a whole other era, not to mention a whole other person—"

Joe hands Diane her yoyo and surges to his feet, saying, "Let's go out on the porch. It's easier to show you there." Tracy casts Ellen a look as she follows Joe, but Diane only has eyes for him.

After they are out of earshot, Ellen puts her feet up on the coffee table and says, "Touchy, huh?"

"That didn't seem to stop you."

"Mom, if we paid attention to Joe's moods, we'd be afraid to say anything."

"He's not that bad."

"Joe and I know how to take one another. Our insensitivity to one another's feelings is a cherished privilege."

"If you say so."

"Anyway, how long has this guy been asleep?"

"That can't be me you're referring to." Michael is standing halfway up the stairs.

"Shit," says Ellen. "There you are!" and she runs up the steps and grabs him around the waist and starts kissing him, pulling him down the stairs. Michael laughs and it is true, her abandon is delightful. She is no happier to see him than the rest of us are, but she makes us seem doubtful by contrast. She pulls him over to the couch, where she sits beside him and throws her leg over his. "Well, damn," she says. "I lived these two years completely without you, and it didn't cause me a moment's pain, and now, looking at you, I can't understand how I got through a single day. How was it? What was the best thing?"

"Well, the Himalayas were a pretty good thing. I saw two tigers."

"You're kidding! How was the food?"

"Good, good—"

"What was the best thing?"

"The best food? It wasn't—"

"Well, in two years there must have been a memorable meal. When Jerry and I were in England—"

"It's not like England, the food—"

"God, I can't believe you're here! Can you?"

He pauses before answering her, just looking. She says, "If you're going to say there was no good food, I'd believe you. You look terrible." She lifts his shirt and gazes at his abdomen, then squeezes his upper arm. He says, "You want a look at my teeth?"

"You've still got some?" Then she leans forward and kisses him tenderly on the cheek.

Joe reappears, sits back down on the piano bench, plays a few notes on the piano, pretends not to see Michael. He says, "How's the picnic coming, Mom? I'm getting a little hungry."

"It's ready. We just have to put it in the car."

"Where are you going?" says Ellen.

"Eagle Point Park."

"Mmmp."

"What does that mean?" says Joe.

"It means mmmp." She heaves herself out of the couch. It means, I bet, that she is miffed at not having been asked along. She pinches Joe on the cheek and says, "I think you are so cute."

He smooches his lips sarcastically at her. Then she strokes Michael on the hair and says, "Bye, sweetie. I love you." For me, there is, as usual, no recognition of parting, not even a wave. Joe follows her out, to say goodbye to the girls.

Michael leans forward and looks at me. He says, "Hey, Mom. Have you ever seen any movies by Satyajit Ray?"

"I don't think so."

"I think I need to show about ten of those movies before I can talk about it."

"But you don't have to have anything to say about INDIA, Michael. Just about what it seemed like to you."

"But that's the point. It isn't possible to have your own feelings about India, or even Benares. It's almost not even possible to have a point of view. If I talk, I'll just hear myself say what everyone says." He leans back and closes his eyes, then says, "Actually, I have more thoughts about America now than India. I mean, one weird thing about Americans is the way they talk as if what they want actually has significance."

"Doesn't it? I mean, Kroger's, four-lane highways, missile silos?"

"I don't mean significant in that what they want could happen, but that they assume it SHOULD happen."

"Don't Indians think that what they want should happen?"

"Not really. I mean, some think it might happen, and some think it won't happen, and some think it better happen."

"I don't think that's so different."

"It is different."

"What is different?" Joe flops into a chair, casual. Michael closes his eyes and drops his head on the back of the couch. "India. What else? Anyway, the worst thing about living abroad is that you spend the whole time talking about it, sort of regarding yourselves in this new place. It's all anyone talks about for weeks at a time. People who've been there for years still talk about it. Nobody gets any closer to understanding it. It's more like constantly looking in a mirror than real conversation."

I say, "I thought you met people you liked there."

"There were people I loved there." He sighs.

Joe pushes his fingers through his hair and gazes off toward the bookcases. He says, "Anybody hungry?"

Michael goes on. "I mean, Ma, I don't have many thoughts about it. All I have is this little accumulation of things that I remember saying that sounded pretty clever at the time, and most of those things I said in letters."

"I didn't earn many letters, it's true."

"But you must have read Joe's."

I shake my head.

Michael says, "Oh."

Joe turns elaborately from the bookcases to me. "I didn't realize I was supposed to be passing them around. They seemed pretty personal."

"Well, not too personal for Mom."

"Oh," says Joe.

"Who's hungry?" I say. "It's nearly five. I'm going to step into the shower for a moment." Anxiety accumulates, one grain at a time, in my chest.

In the shower, I think some more about Michael's remark. On Thursday the federal government brought suit against the state to repair some roads in the southern part of the state, and to build a new four-lane connecting the Naval Weapons Support Center to Interstate 68. It is a remote and beautiful part of the state—good-sized hills and a number of national forests. The rumor is that the navy plans to store disintegrating chemical weapons there. It will be my job for the DOT, maybe as early as Monday, to say that we don't have the money. This is a budgetary fiction on the order of imagining that I control a large jar full of cash, and that I can tell by counting the cash what the state can afford. Money (or at least the figures in my department's computers) seems to the public and even to the politicians to be a fact they can appeal to that will tell them what they really want. The fact is that they can have anything they really want. That's what the lawyers in Washington know. They know that they can make us build the roads, that they can even make us want the roads, and that the way to do that is to sue us. If we come up with sufficient strength of argument against these roads, then they will see that making us want what they want is too difficult, and they will store those chemical weapons elsewhere.

It is finding out what we want that takes time, effort, and money. From the top right down through my department and the environmental groups, no one knows what we want or how much we want it. I happen to know that the rumors that the navy intends to store something dangerous at the facility, and thus transport it over our roads and through our towns to get it there, originated in the office of one of

the lawyers pressing the federal suit. I know that the environmental groups knew about the suit the day it was filed, because two of my accountants called people they knew from college and told them about it. Is this corruption? Is this conscience? I think it is a way that Americans have of discovering what they really want. On Monday I will probably say, "I don't see how the DOT is going to afford seventy miles of new interstate with the state budget in the shape it's in," and everybody will be reassured by the figures, the facts. But the decisive questions are: How much does the navy want it? How much does the state not want it?

In my experience, there is only one motivation, and that is desire. No reasons or principles contain it or stand against it. The rumor was that it took my mother's cousin nine years to save up the money for her escape to Denver, and she did it in a world where women carried no money. Another cousin of my mother's persuaded her father to let her go to the local day college during the Depression. She got a scholarship for tuition, and found another student who was willing to drive her to school, but the uncle in question refused all money for books. She would stand in the stacks of the library, near the study carrels of students she recognized from her classes. When they got up to take breaks or chat, she would read the textbooks they had left lying open. When I used to tell this story to the children (demonstrating how much someone could desire an education), they would each try it, declare it impossible. But there was no doubting Cousin Maia. Even as a child, I never questioned the power of desire.

When I come down from my shower, Joe and Michael are on the floor by the stereo, going through Joe's new records (he combs the secondhand stores). Michael is animated and appreciative, and I can see that Joe is pleased. He plays songs from different albums, but listen to this, wait

till you hear this one, and Michael peruses the jackets. They are enjoying themselves in an utterly serious way, trading information. Pretty soon they will be on to baseball. They don't notice me as I step past them into the kitchen, except to move out of the way.

Eagle Point Park is one of my favorite places, and if there is something I have been looking forward to about Michael's return, it is this pleasure. When the hot weather broke last week, my first thought was that it would be nice for this picnic. When I saw that Kroger's had fresh blueberries and late raspberries, I thought, Homemade berry ice cream for the picnic. Maybe because of my farm childhood, I always feel relieved, lightened, in the out of doors. Real festivities, for me, take place alfresco, and I think that, when I am sitting in my favorite stone park shelter, across from Michael on a hard wooden bench, then I will realize that he is back, that there are dangers he has encountered and overcome, and I will throw off this practical caution about his return and be exhilarated.

I begin to feel it as Joe drives through the stone gates and turns down one of the park roads. He says, "The usual, Ma?" The usual is in a glade overlooking the creek. The path along the creek winds past it. "You bet," I say.

Joe says, "Mom is such a creature of habit."

We hurriedly pile the picnic things on the table and set out down the leftward path, toward a small series of waterfalls in an especially shaded and pleasant stretch of woods. Two can walk on the path abreast. I follow them. After I have paused a few times to identify flowers with the book I am carrying, they are well ahead of me, chatting comfortably.

It is obvious from a distance that Joe is cheering up. His surprised, barking laugh sounds once, then again and again. Although he specializes in irony and rue, he can give himself

up to fun quite suddenly and completely, and in fact one of the things Louise said in the letter I read was that she'd never had so much fun with anyone as with Joe. I stop and let them get out of sight, then slip off my shoes and step into the water. It is shallow and warm, but glassy. My toes look large and bleached against the ancient bronze pebbles of the creek bed. The creek has that perfect peaceful flow—without turbulence and clear, almost silent. When a twig or a leaf scoots past, its velocity seems improbable. The creek on my mother's farm was a rope of water winding through turf, visible from the distance as a dark loop in the tawny landscape. Here and there, cottonwoods clumped beside it, and on the neighboring farm, it widened into a small slough. Every year, in the slough, there were waves of ducks and geese and pheasants and prairie chickens, but even the creek on the farm was teeming with insects and birds and rodents and rabbits and foxes. This creek is more like a photograph, with artfully scattered rocks, arching green limbs, and a stone bridge built by the CCC. Except for water spiders and midges, I've never seen any wildlife, but it is always refreshing to come here. I wade to the middle of the creek and climb onto a flat rock that gives me a view down the tunnel of leaves. Two weeks ago they were still and dusty with summer, but rain last week appears to have perked them up. I am satisfied with this.

I never thought I would be. What I longed for on the farm was not Chicago, not streets or the lighted windows of Marshall Field's, but vertiginous landscape; certainly mountains, necessarily waterfalls, and preferably dazzling icecaps and crashing surf. I had a list of places I would not die without visiting: New Zealand, Norway, Alaska, Japan and the mountains of southern China, Peru. When I was fourteen, a discontented age, I carried this list in my pocket, and spent a lot of time fixing upon just the right order for my visits, and just the right amount of time to spend in

each place. It was never less than three months. I envisioned myself drinking in the landscape day after day, never failing to respond to it with every nerve ending. Sometimes during my marriage this longing would reassert itself, though Pat felt that it was decadent to long for the picturesque, and I would plan trips, and even make reservations, for places like Kyoto and Auckland. We did get to the Grand Canyon, Pike's Peak, and the Blue Ridge Mountains. Since the divorce I haven't gone anywhere except for business trips to Washington and camping here and there in some of the state parks. In the last few years, I have even had the money, at least for a tour to Norway.

I could say that the terror of my divorce and its aftermath tamed me, made me an accountant to my very soul, when I could have become a bush pilot or a naturalist, or I could say, like most people, that I simply couldn't get away. The truth seems to me more delicate, having more to do with how lovely this spot is, how I need to see it develop through the seasons, and not only this spot but three or four others, all within an hour's drive of my house. The joke is on me, who has turned out to have that farmer's attachment to familiar places, after all.

When I get back to the shelter in the dusk, Joe and Michael have set out the food and are ready to eat. Michael, in fact, is already eating.

Michael is saying, "So here was this guy, classic math nerd. The operative variable with Stanley was that he had gone through the New York City school system, and so he had skipped all these grades, and when he got to our school in India, he was about nineteen. He talked a lot about how he was going to be a hard grader, and a rigorous teacher, so the kids were pretty scared, and about the time of his final exam for the term, people began coming to his office, or students would catch him before class, and they would give him a brass plate, or a dish of mangoes. Stanley didn't

see anything unusual in this. I guess he'd gotten presents all his life, and he was in the habit of feeling entitled to them. So he gave the exam, and graded hard, and prided himself on separating the friendship he felt for the students from professionalism, and the day after the grades went out, there was practically a riot in the school when all the parents showed up in a rage. And the guy never understood. He never understood that he'd accepted bribes and not upheld his end of the bargain."

Joe says, "Didn't you tell him?"

"Oh, by his time I wasn't doing much with the Americans. And anyway, he was such a know-it-all that, when you tried to suggest anything to him, he just got red in the face and started panting. He hated me."

"I had this girl in my history of science class," says Joe, "who always sat in the front row, right in front of me, and one day she just started to unbutton her blouse. She looked right at me and pushed the buttons through the holes like they were lollipops or something."

"Or something." They laugh.

"I was standing at the board, and when I sat down behind my desk, she gave me this big smile, like I'd gotten an erection all of a sudden."

"Had you?"

"Well—" They laugh.

I say, "So what'd you do?"

"I waited until she was all done, and broke the class into small groups. You never saw a shirt buttoned so fast in your life."

Michael dishes some fruit salad onto my plate, then unwraps a marinated-tofu-and-avocado sandwich for me. He says, "I bet life in the bureaucracy is pretty tame compared to this."

"There was the shoe guy."

"Who was that?"

"No one knew, actually. Every so often this well-dressed man would appear, and he would go up to women in back hallways or get them alone in the elevator and beg to lick the bottom of their shoes. He wasn't threatening or anything, but he would just plead and whine, until these women found themselves letting him do it."

Joe says, "It was probably the governor." We all laugh.

"No one ever knew if it was even a state employee. No one recognized him, and it only happened three or four times. There was a plan about what we would do, but he never showed up after we made it."

I eat. Michael tells another story, then Joe tells one. Dusk is gathering, and I can hear the creek running under the sound of their voices. The exhilaration of Michael's homecoming begins to grip me. It is wonderful to converse like this, as if there were no underlying expectations supplied by the filial relationship.

I look away from them, out into the darkness under the trees, maybe to look away from the thought I have just had, which is that I may never see that phenomenon again that always struck me in the old days, that even their bodies, especially their bodies, were duplicates. I didn't think about it much until they were about three and their little nakednesses began to take shape. Moles on the left side of their necks, square chests, thin calves. Later, when they were seven, pigeon breasts, long arms, big hands, big feet. Always two or four of everything. They were handsome little boys, who stood up straight, did not fidget. I would have been proud of one, as I was proud of the other ones. But I admit it, my pride was magnified by how identical they were. As I sit on this hard bench, I suddenly yearn for one last long look, and not only of the phenomenon of little Joe and little Michael, but of the others, too: Ellen, four, and Annie, seven months, sharing a peach; Daniel, two or three, rolling from one end of the living room to the other until

he was dizzy, then standing up and shouting, "There she goes!", meaning that the room was spinning. As I watch Joe watch Michael shovel in the food, that fact that I will never see their toddler selves again is tormenting.

"You know," says Joe. "I looked up this condition of yours in the encyclopedia while you were sleeping. It's not something I want to share, all things considered. It can go to the liver, or even the lungs."

"In India, people have it all their lives. It's not the worst thing. I do need a prescription, though, because you can't buy the right drugs over the counter here like you can there."

"I take it these drugs suppress the symptoms without really getting at the little buggers." Joe sounds annoyed.

"I don't know."

"Go to the doctor."

"I said I was going to, didn't I?"

Talk subsides. The evening insects have begun to buzz and saw. A light breeze begins to sound in the leaves, drowning out the sigh of the water. I roll up my paper plate and fold the ends over.

Joe says, "So, we'll go get Barbara and Kevin, and try Caruso's? They have a good pianist Saturday nights. There's a jazz trio at Handy's, too."

"Sounds good. Did you call Barbara?"

They are going out.

Why not?

But it takes my breath away all the same.

"Just for a few hours, Mom. No big deal, okay?"

"No big deal."

Michael looks up from his bowl of raspberry-blueberry ice cream. They are staring at me, gauging whether they have hurt my feelings. They have, though I didn't expect them to, and I would rather they didn't know it. I say, pushing up from the picnic table, "Michael, you should call

your father, too." The fact is that, though I now feel envious and excluded, after they go I will be myself again, alone in the silence of my house, books, knitting, TV, bed, laundry, for that matter. I was an only child who grew up on a farm. I have been entertaining myself successfully for fifty-two years. Actually, I will put on some music of my own. It will be an old recording of Jussi Bjoerling singing famous tenor solos. And in places, I will sing along. A thin plan. When people leave, they always seem to scoop themselves out of you. I wonder why I pay so much attention to my feelings, why Joe does, why Michael and Ellen do. We are like those scientists that Joe talks about, always stopping in the road to contemplate boulders, except that the boulders aren't anything interesting, like the speed of light or the nature of gravity, they are only the rubble of our own feelings.

My punishment for having reacted is to endure Joe's apologetic scrutiny all the way back to the house, then his oh-so-careful help putting away the picnic things.

Michael is on the phone with the controversial fifth man. There is the scrape of a chair as he sits down to talk. I climb the stairs and feel a sudden weird contentment at the familiarity of this, as if I could cherish the last twenty years after all.

The fact is that Pat and I did not part peacefully. We did not behave well in any sense. The opening scene of the long drama that was our parting took place just about exactly twenty years ago. We were in the newly remodeled kitchen of our house in the country. The cabinets were new. The flooring was new. At my insistence, windows had been cut into the walls on the southern and eastern exposures. The ceiling and the appliances were new. I had been conducting this remodeling for seven months—I thought then, to give our life a suitable domestic container. Five months into the remodeling, I fell in love with a neighbor, a writer who was

home a good deal during the day. His entrance onto the scene, I thought at the time, was unaccountable, for the simple reason that with five children, a demanding husband, a mother in ill health, and a major remodeling, I couldn't possibly have had time for him. I made time for him. Then, one Saturday night in the kitchen, with the younger children in bed and the older ones sleeping out for the night, I saw that what I had been building was a set for the play that was about to begin. Pat and I were the main characters, the writer, whose name was Ed, had a crucial part, and the kitchen, the kitchen represented, in its passing moment of completeness, what was about to be dismantled. What was about, I should say, to be detonated.

Michael and Joe were five and a half, and were about to enter kindergarten. The older children had been in school until three every day before the summer, and were now in summer day camp. All day long, every day, for almost a year, it had been the boys and me. The house and the five-acre yard made up a world for us, and it seems to me that I remember from my own childhood that thick, surrounding quality that such worlds have. The yard was full of old plantings—flowering bushes, beds of tiger lilies, lilac trees, patches of iris, spirea bunched everywhere. A stream ran not far from the house, and there was a long sledding hill between the house and the road. For an entire year, between eight and three every weekday, my sons and I lived an idyllic domestic life. The fall was colorful, the snow was deep, the spring wet, the vegetation just at eye level for them. The world was full of secure hiding places, the demanding older children were gone, they had me, they had each other. Passing completeness. It was no fiction, this complete daily world. For those hours of the day I was happy and productive and as pleased with my sons as they were with me. Two mornings a week that summer they went to nursery school—Pat's idea, to encourage other friends and the be-

ginnings of independence from each other. I left the con-
tractors in the house and walked down the gravel road to
Ed's place. It was an old, old house, three rooms and a
summer kitchen out back with a potbellied stove cast in
1884. Ed was winterizing it, and to me it had the austere
glamour of temporary shelter, like a tent pitched at fourteen
thousand feet.

A Saturday night during the Johnson Administration.
Man and wife, woman and husband, protagonist and an-
tagonist, victim and perpetrator, were standing not far from
one another. He was wearing a light blue shirt and slacks,
opening the refrigerator to take out the milk. She was wearing her pink seersucker bathrobe, and was standing, hands
on hips, near the sink. Aside from the light of the refrigerator, only one other light was on, that above the sink.
For a moment, in the general gloom of the room, they were
both lit up, and at that moment she said, "Pat, I have been
having a relationship with Ed Stackhouse, down the road,
and I am not going to stop. It is a sexual relationship, and
a friendship, too."

Of course my intentions had something vague and un-
realistic to do with Ed; I wouldn't have had the courage to
speak otherwise. Pat did not take the milk out. He closed
the refrigerator door and strode over, glass still in hand. He
looked staggered and I knew that I had caught him by surprise, for the first time ever. I felt myself relent, as if my
vertebrae were unhooking, and I opened my mouth to say
something less resolute, when he slapped me so hard across
the face that I fell to the month-old flooring. Then he threw
the glass against one of the new windows, cracking it and
smashing the glass.

On Sunday afternoon there was a tremendous thunder-
storm, with pounding rain, thunder crashing and lightning
striking almost continuously. There was so much noise
from the storm that you couldn't hear the sirens warning

of nearby tornadoes. We were in the basement of the house, huddled under the workbench, for an hour and a half. Pat did not either speak to me or look at me, but we had been married so long that each of us knew exactly how to move, exactly what to expect of the other, how, together, to manage as well as comfort the children. For dinner we ate canned hash; then we put the children to bed. When he was sure they were all asleep, he took me into the kitchen and said, his hands balled into fists at his sides, that he expected me to take my clothes and leave in the morning, after everyone was gone, that if he found me when he came home at noon, he would kill me. As if to make sure that I believed him, he knocked me down again. I believed him. I thought, though, that if I agreed to what he wanted, and gave him time to cool off, he would accept a new life. Others we knew had divorced. Everyone knew it was hard. But the agreements that those couples labored to achieve looked inevitable to the rest of us.

In the morning I kissed Ellen and Daniel and Annie and put them on the day-camp bus with a smile. Annie was to have riding that day; Ellen and Daniel, canoeing. I remember every piece of clothing I found for them. I dressed Michael and Joe. I kissed them. They got into the back seat of the Pontiac. I stood back. Pat rolled down his window. As he was letting out the emergency brake, he looked at me and said, "I mean it."

I was too proud to call Ed just then. Besides, I suspected that he would disapprove. I went to a friend's house. On Tuesday, when I called, Pat seemed exhausted but reasonable. He said, "The children were very upset, so I told them your mother had gotten sick again and you'd gone to take care of her. I said you'd be back Sunday. Can we leave it this way for now, and talk Sunday?" I was disarmed by his questioning me, touched by the fatigue, rare and human for Pat. I spent the next few days weighing the two of him,

murderous, forgiving, unable really to believe that our parting could go smoothly, but ready to accept that piece of
luck if it were available. It never occurred to me to doubt
his good intentions, though. The next Sunday, when I called
to suggest a time for my return and a strategy for telling
the children, I got a disconnect message. I jumped in my
car and raced over to the house. It was empty, with a "For
Sale" sign at the bottom of the drive. When I phoned the
realtor at his home, he said, "Lovely house, three baths.
You don't usually find that in one of these older homes.
Completely redone, country kitchen. Sold it already. But
I have others I can show you." Monday morning I drove
in a panic to the day camp, but they were gone. Ellen,
Daniel, Annie—nowhere among the riders or the swim-
mers or the canoers or the children making lanyards out of
plastic string. I went to the director, making public for the
first time the rift in our family, and said, "Where are the
Kinsella children?"

"Aren't you Mrs. Kinsella?"

"Well, yes."

"Dr. Kinsella informed us early last week that the children
would be leaving for their vacation over the weekend." And
she stared at me, unable to mask her confusion. Well, she
wasn't the last official that I questioned to find out where
my children were, and those children at their activities were
only the first groups that I scanned for familiar faces in the
course of the next four years. In the afternoon mail was a
note from Pat, saying that he had accepted a position in a
teaching hospital elsewhere, and that he was enclosing a
check for a thousand dollars. The receptionist at Pat's lab
said that, yes, he had gone on vacation, and then would be
taking a leave of absence. His secretary came on the line
after a pause, and said, "Is that you, Mrs. K.?"

"Yes, Donna."

"Did you know about all this? He said you did, but I wondered."

Now it was my turn to pause. "No, Donna."

"You don't know where he's going, or anything?"

"No."

"Oh, Lord." And she hung up.

And what about Ed? It is true that he didn't know where I was for that week, and must have seen the sign go up on our front lawn. When I called to make a date with him, a lunch date for talking because I was afraid of anything else, he accepted, it seemed to me, with relief that bordered on enthusiasm. The next day he called and said that we wouldn't be seeing each other anymore, even to talk. I had admired the single-minded focus that allowed Ed to write a novel about Alaska in the morning and a book about the White House in the afternoon, so there was a way in which I had to admire the fact that he never spoke to me again.

It was said of people in concentration camps that, if they could not believe that what had happened to them was possible, then they were more likely to die quickly, as if of incredulity. It was true of me that incredulity slowed my mental processes nearly to a halt; in fact, those early days were so strange I didn't recognize them as mine, much less make plans, devise tactics. I might have thought of my aunt, "down to Norfolk in the State Home," who must have considered her new circumstances as changeless and beyond her power as mine seemed. I didn't, though. I had no thoughts, only a bright inner glare, the afterimage of a huge explosion imprinted on the retina. I had left in my blue Corvair with a suitcase of clothes. The rest of my life—children, dogs, house, furniture, mementos, books, pots and pans—went out of my possession like smoke.

About a month later, I got a slip of paper in the mail. It was typed, and it read, "12, Marlboro Crescent, London

S.W. 11, England." It was my first week at a job that it had taken me all of that time to find, typing in the business school at the university. The thousand dollars was used up on the lawyer I had hired to find the children and get them back, the joint bank accounts were closed. My paycheck, eighty-nine dollars per week, covered my rent and my food and the lawyer's long distance phone bills. The children might as well have been at the South Pole. It took me nine months and a blizzard of letters to persuade Pat to let me even visit them. He must have heard from friends that I was poverty-stricken and gaunt, that Ed had stopped speaking to me, that I didn't seem to have a new boyfriend, that I had been utterly humbled.

Well, I hadn't been humbled at all, but I had been reduced to a few clear positions. One of these was relief at the end of married life, the dawn of privacy; another was resolve upon a professional degree and a good job. The third was at least partial custody of at least some of my children. The clarity of these goals and the fact that I was dead to the past gave me one advantage over Pat, who was in a turmoil of longing and fury over what had been lost and how to make it again with another woman. He was a wily and powerful adversary, smarter than I was, as always. I had been foolish to tell him about Ed, foolish to drive away without the children, foolish to hire the inexperienced lawyer that I could afford, foolish to underestimate Pat's desire for revenge. In court, his lawyer made "their removal to England" sound responsible, extraction from an unstable and immoral situation.

More than once I thought he would kill me. In his lawyer's office one time, he lunged across the table at me, and his lawyer, a burly ex-rower, had to grab him by the coat and then the shoulders and pull him back. I stood there without blinking, small and hard and ready to be killed. By that time I was ready for anything, as ferociously attentive

as a marten or a mink—one of those small, vicious northern animals that can never be tamed. For courage, I reminded myself that I had caught him unawares once.

I ceased being surprised at what people are capable of, ceased longing for Pat's explanation, or Ed's, or even the opportunity to say one last thing, reach one last understanding. And Pat's passion ended. It got increasingly convenient for him to let me have more of the children. Joe, whiny then, shy and hard to please, lived with me most of the time. Daniel went through a period of bad behavior—low grades, smoking marijuana, drinking and driving—and was shipped to me in a hurry. Annie spent her sullen stages at my house. With Ellen, Pat was locked in battle. When she made herself horrible enough, he sent her to me. Michael was the prize, Pat's favorite boy. For years he almost never came, and then it was only the accident and Pat's burgeoning new family that made it possible. As for separating identical twins, he considered that a positive good, and supported his position with statistics about test scores and theories about brain development. His intention, he said, was to overcome for them the disadvantage of having been born twins, and, furthermore, it was Joe, smaller by a pound at birth, always subordinate and dependent, who would benefit the most from leading his own life. He dismissed my arguments that Joe needed Michael, missed him, yearned for him.

I took what I could get, knowing that, according to the custody agreement, the choice was his. Tatty had babies. I dated Simon Elliott. One by one, the children went to college and graduated and got jobs and mates and even children, and we all got to the point where our ancient agitations were unrecognizable even to ourselves. And unrecognizable, too, my passion for Ed Stackhouse, what his austere little house and travel tales aroused in me. Above his kitchen table was a map of the world, and it was covered with pins,

designating places he had visited. Now that I can hardly remember what he looked like or what his bed was like, I'm sure that what I really wanted was not to love him but to be him.

It is nearly midnight when I come down to turn on the hall light. The ground floor is dark—Joe would have thriftily turned out the lights upon leaving—and I don't bother to turn them on when I go into the dining room and the kitchen to open a few windows to the evening breeze. A dark shape dozing at one end of the couch, I realize before I have the sense to grow afraid, is Ellen. Her head lies back, exposing her neck, and her breathing ruffles with a low snore. All the windows in the room are up, and magazine covers have blown open, papers have slid from my desk to the carpeting. I'm annoyed enough to consider touching her naked throat and startling her, but she is too quick for me. She says, "What time IS it?" sits up, and stretches.

"I didn't know you were here."

"All the lights were off. I figured you had gone out with Joe and Michael. I did call up the stairs. What were you doing up there?" Her tone is immediately challenging.

"Knitting. Reading. Listening to music."

"The stereo down here is better. You've got this whole big house—"

"Which means that I can sit in my room sometimes."

"The doors were wide open. Anyone could—"

"Is the front door unlocked? And the side door, too? I told Joe—"

"Well—"

"Well?"

"Well, actually, I came in the back, after trying the other doors. Didn't you hear the Malones' dogs barking in their pen?"

"No, and I didn't hear the doorbell ring, either."

She ignores this, reaches for the lamp behind her. Its glow reveals that, though her hair is combed, her face is a little puffy. Sweatshirt, no shoes. She says, "Want some ice cream?" and goes into the kitchen.

There is something to be made of this, but I am not going to be the one to make it. Ellen's unannounced appearance in my house is nothing remarkable, even this late at night, so I am not going to remark upon other signs. On her way to the kitchen, she flips every light switch she passes, a habit she has always had that I suppose is like my own feeling that lots of unused rooms are welcoming. She likes the most distant corners to be ready for her.

She brings back the canister of berry-berry ice cream and two spoons, already diving in, saying with her mouth full, "Mmm. This is good, Mom. You must have made it for your picnic." There will be more to this. There is. "I bet it was nice, huh."

"Same as always. That's a nice spot."

"Too bad you couldn't have had a larger group."

I lick my lips, hiding a tiny smile, then say, "I'm not sure Michael is up to larger groups."

"Why is everyone acting like this trip is some long illness that he's recuperating from? How are they getting along, anyway?"

"Fine, I think. They went out with Kevin and Barbara."

"The senator and his wife?"

"The very same."

"Feel a little left out?" She catches my gaze over the rim of the ice cream canister and holds it. I cock my head, a type of shrug. She grins happily and sits down, lifts her feet to the edge of the coffee table. She says, conversational now rather than needling, "Jennifer is spending the night."

"You finally gave in, then."

"She is so literal-minded. All day long Diane just stood

back and watched while Jennifer asked questions. What time
is bedtime at your house, Ellen? Is that go-upstairs time, or
lights-out time, or go-to-sleep time? Can I get up to go to
the bathroom if I want to? Can I get a drink, or should I
call you? Is there a glass for me in the bathroom? Where
is it?"

I chuckle.

"I looked at her when I was tucking her in, and I thought,
Joe would say this is the real thing, so I said, 'Do you want
a kiss good night, Jennifer?' and she said, 'Do you mean on
the lips or on the cheek?' Diane is in love."

I put my feet up on the coffee table and reach a spoon
into the ice cream. So. Okay. I am lucky that there is always
this comfort to come back to, this incidental bumping on
the couch of mother and daughter, this expectation of conversation like silk running through your hands. I admit I
am often amused and sometimes annoyed at Ellen's rudeness, but this is what she is aiming for, this rare comfort
between mother and daughter. It might be that we would
not have had it had our history been more conventional.
As a child she was disputatious and resolute, with a will to
have the last word that sometimes bordered on the self-
destructive. After Pat brought the children back from England, Ellen embarked upon her mythic wars against his
tyranny. At the same time he was fighting me in court for
full custody and had twice moved the children secretly so
that I couldn't get in touch with them, Ellen hounded and
disobeyed him so relentlessly that she won herself pretty
free access to me, and when he moved away to Chicago, a
year before the accident, she moved in with me and Joe. I
was the spoils of war, and she cherished me accordingly. I
felt the same about her, I have to admit. She enjoyed the
added conviction that the war had been hers and she had
won it; I was grateful for my good luck. Her years with
me were delightful—no fights, no teen-age resentment—

but I have since thought that she trained herself for a different life from the one she has chosen, and that she has never quite figured out how to beat her swords into plowshares. But I don't know. The little girl I remember? When she was four, she insisted that she never slept. When I doubted her about it, she spent a month calling to me at all hours of the night, announcing what time it was and declaring that she was wide awake.

I try to accept the mystery of my children, of the inexplicable ways they diverge from parental expectations, of how, however much you know or remember of them, they don't quite add up.

Sunday morning I am dressed and rummaging through the pantry as the eastern windows begin to lighten, and I see that it is going to be another lovely morning, hot afternoon. The long grass lies over, gray with moisture. I decide to go out and pick some marigolds for the kitchen table, and my sneakers leave dark tracks in the dew. The Malones cut their lawn yesterday, as every Saturday—there is still a sweet grassy smell lingering in the air, and the marigolds, as I bend down to cut them, give off an intense odor—sweet-acrid—that some people hate but that I love. In Nebraska, of course, my mother's farm garden was huge and important—rows of cabbages and tomatoes and potatoes and brussels sprouts and turnips, but all of them separated by thick lines of orange and brown marigolds or brightly colored nasturtiums. I press the cushiony little blossoms to my face. Behind me—I don't have to turn and look, I know what is there—my house is full of sleep.

Well, the fact is that I have been a mother for thirty years, now, half again longer than I was a child, and the last thirty years have given me as many habits and predilections as my childhood did. The bodies in the house, whose presence

comforts me, are the bodies of my children, not my mother and father. What comforts me is not my own safety anymore, but theirs.

I have learned, over the last twenty years, to embrace the possible and not to mourn the rest. I don't often think, as I did last night, of those little five-and-a-half-year-old boys, climbing so trustfully into the back seat of the blue Pontiac. Michael in blue shorts and white T-shirt, carrying a toy metal cement mixer, a crescent-shaped scab on his knee, Joe in khaki shorts and green striped T-shirt, a pad of paper and a short pencil sticking out of his pocket. Even as I turn my attention to Pat, I hear Michael say, "17 plus 27," and Joe reply, at once, "44." Joe looks at Michael and smiles, Michael looks at me, attentive, knowing that there is something wrong with me. But that thick, solid world still surrounds them. Their bodies move confidently, expressing the knowledge that the back seat is theirs, the Pontiac is theirs, the house and the yard and the mom and the dad are theirs. They fidget and settle, ready to get started, and, without a backward glance, they are driven into the unknowable future.

I look toward the house. Long shafts of light blaze up the yellow siding, casting the black shadows of the chestnut trees against the porch; the screen door swings slowly on its hinges; squirrels jump from roof to tree limb then run headlong at the ground. The dew evaporates in the rising sun. Right now they are safe here, in my house, taking, as they think, care of me. Isn't that a picture to set beside the other one, a picture of survival next to a picture of betrayal? Don't they cancel each other out? My pleasure in this morning, this ordinary beauty, prods me to think they do.

It must be about eight-thirty when Joe comes down, dressed, Bertrand Russell in his hand. As always, he goes straight to the coffee machine, prepares and downs his first

half-cup, smacks his lips over it. "Hi, Mom," he says, affectionately.

"Hi, sweetie."

"Didn't get in too late, Mom."

"Did you have a good time?"

"Okay, I guess. Yeah, it was okay." He stirs his coffee, resting his head in his hand. Oh, he is so moody. He says, "I don't think Michael had a very good time. I feel responsible for that."

"Why?"

"Well, going out was my idea. It's no big deal." He picks up the shredded-wheat box and pours some into his bowl. I put the milk on the table, then go back to pouring cake batter into the layer tins.

"I mean," Joe goes on, "he sounds like he has tuberculosis or something. You should hear him up in the bathroom. I've never heard such coughing and throat-clearing in my whole life. I peeked in. I could swear I saw him inhale water out of his hands into his nose and then spit it into the sink. Mom, I don't think I know this guy."

"He does seem to be coughing a lot."

"Last night the pianist was having a break, and Barbara started talking about her dog-training class, and it was pretty funny, and Kevin and I were laughing—you know how Barbara tells a story; she can make growing tomatoes on her front porch sound like a three-ring circus. Anyway, Kevin and I were cracking up, and I looked over at Michael and he was smiling, I mean, his smile was at the table but he wasn't. And right when I was watching, he got farther away, like he couldn't bear us or something. And I caught myself thinking, Training dogs? Children are starving! All that crap."

"He must be pretty tired."

"You're right. I'm sorry." He gets up and pours himself

people—slide in and out of his manner, reminding but not convincing me to change my expectations of him. I don't think Joe is even reminded, because Michael is careful to be his old self around his twin. Or maybe Joe brings that out in him. At any rate, he is back to being perky and ironic when Joe sits down again. "Hey, Mom," Joe says. "Guess what."

"What?"

"Kevin has a new job. He's actually an administrative assistant to the state Republican central committee. Can you believe it?"

"I thought he was just working at a temp job researching in the legislative library."

"He WAS. He got that through Manpower. But that was a year ago. Now he's moved up through the ranks."

"That's nice," I say.

"Well," says Joe, "I don't think it's NICE. I think it's weird. And he's been working at this job for four months and he hasn't dared to tell me before this. I think it's base and corrupt."

Michael cocks his head and looks at Joe. I say, "Well—"

"I mean, this is the guy who spray-painted WE ARE VICTORIOUS, U.S. OUT OF VIETNAM, APRIL 23 on the wall of the gymnasium when he was a freshman in high school."

"Was that Kevin?"

"Now you're the only one who knows besides us."

I open my mouth.

"We didn't help," says Michael.

"But we destroyed the paint cans. God, remember that? They all said, Do not puncture or incinerate. I thought they might explode or something. We wore these gloves so we wouldn't get our fingerprints on them. He used to call himself 'the senator' because it was subversive. Now I think he means it. The Republican party, Jesus."

Michael says, "I admire the way he went out and did it,

"No."

"Every month." He smiles knowingly. I feel sheepish. "Almost every month. I never knew what to say. I thought about you every day. And everyone else was writing you all the time."

"I was far away, Mom."

"Not so far." I get up and take his bowl and cup to the sink. He says, "Well, it's true, I was only halfway around the world. If you leave the planet you can get farther."

"It didn't feel far to me. You may not know this, but a mom is never alone, even if none of her kids is in the vicinity."

"So, sit down." His gaze is intent, almost disconcerting. He was jealous as a small child, even of Joe, but especially of anything I would do for Daniel. At two and three he tried every means of wooing me, from the most transparent flattery (Mother's Day was his favorite holiday), to the angriest demands for favor and notice. At four he got into bed on my side every night, rolled right up to me, and put his arms around me. It got so I began wearing my robe to bed and sleeping curled up. Pat said we should draw the line, but Michael's determination was so furious that even he dared not interfere. Finally, after about three months, I started finding Michael in Joe's bed, the top bunk, rolled against him.

I sit down. He says, "Oh, Mom."

"I was thinking this picnic would be fun, but we can do it another time. Would you rather do something else for dinner?"

"We could go to some restaurant and order cups of hot water, then put ketchup in them, and have tomato soup. Eat the free bread. Park across the highway behind the drive-in and watch the movie without sound."

"We could. I don't know that I want to."

He is leaning back in his chair, his arm flung over its crest.

His gaze is steady and considering. He sighs. "There were some people in Benares who came back for a visit about six months ago. They said it would be weird. It is. It's almost unbearable."

"In what way, sweetie?"

"I feel like nothing. Just nothing inside. More than disoriented. Deracinated. But I was like this there, too. For about the last four months. I don't want to go back, at least not to India. I was so glad to leave. But I just want to cry. Is that okay for a guy to say to his mom?"

"Sure."

"I wish we were here alone, sort of. Or that Joe and I were here alone. It doesn't seem to me like it's going to be smooth with him. When I was upstairs and everything was quiet, I couldn't fall into a deep sleep, because something was too overwhelming about it. It seemed like if I gave up and went to sleep, the walls would cave in and all sorts of darkness would just flood me. But I was so tired I couldn't wake up completely and come downstairs. And then I heard Ellen and the girls outside and Joe and you all talking, and that scared me, too. I don't know. I thought it would be hard, and it's harder than I thought. Oh, shit." He curses because it has happened, he has started crying. At first the tears are coursing down his cheeks, but then sobs start to shake him, and he fixes his elbows on the table to still his body. He shakes his head and puts his face in his hands. I think of a few moments ago, when he let me look at him, and I put my fingers in his hair and take hold, gripping, but not pulling. It is what my mother used to do to me when I was a child, and I found it oddly comforting.

But to comfort my weeping son, who went to India a boy and returned a man, makes me self-conscious. I grip his hair more tightly, and finally he says, "Ma, you're hurting me." His voice sounds ironic, normal. He takes his hands down from his face. I take my fingers out of his hair.

•

instead of studying it, you know? I mean, most of these old lefties just end up going to graduate school in political science or something. I think he'll ending up actually knowing something."

"I think he'll end up actually knowing nothing." Joe's voice is tight. "Knowing less than nothing—knowing something wrong and thinking it's right."

Michael is casual but disbelieving. "Contaminated just by brushing against a few Republicans?"

"Assisting in smoky rooms is not just brushing against. It's being paid, what, fifteen, eighteen thousand? Blood money."

I say, "Wasn't it the Democrats who gathered in all the smoky rooms?"

"Bullshit." Michael's tone is harsh suddenly.

Joe is startled. He sits back in his chair, panting a little, staring at Michael. Michael pushes the hair off his forehead. "You know what blood money is? I saw what it is in India. It's when somebody is caught for hoarding food in a town that's starving to death, and he pays a little bribe, and gets to keep what he's got and get more, and the people actually starve to death. It's when the police are paid to look the other way when some people decide to go and teach some Sikhs a lesson by burning them up in their houses. I don't think working for the Republican party qualifies Kevin for the lowest circle of political hell by any means."

"Okay, how is Kevin going to be any different in twenty years from those Union Carbide guys who were all over the media, making apologies and excuses about the Bhopal thing? You must have seen them."

"What's this all about? I don't see the connection. It's just a crummy job in state government is all. I don't think you're being very logical, frankly." He tips his chair back. He is being very cool.

Joe is not. "I'm always logical, actually. It's you that can't see the connection, but the connection is there, all right. Do you think those guys knowingly speak lies? Of course not. They wouldn't be effective that way. They actually believe what they are saying, about the good intentions of the company, and the deep sorrow that the CEO feels about the tragedy. The company makes them that way, by bringing them in and training them."

"The CEO probably is sorry."

"He's scared shitless that his insurance rates are going to go through the ceiling is what he is."

"What are we arguing about?"

Joe is sweating. Michael is, too, a little. Joe says, "There's nothing wrong with graduate school."

Michael shrugs. They sit silently, not looking at each other. Finally, Joe jumps up and says, "I'm going to cut the back now," and bangs out of the house. After a moment I say to Michael, "Want anything else?"

"No. Yes. A glass of water. I'll get it." But he continues to sit, only tipping his chair forward. He says, "Hey, Mom. Get this. I didn't even realize we were arguing until almost the end. I couldn't see it. I couldn't see him. He was mad, wasn't he?"

"Almost from the beginning, I'd say."

"Ma, I haven't been mad in two years. I don't know what it feels like, looks like, except when I see it on the street in India, people beating on each other, yelling at each other. I forgot how mad he gets. I mean, during that I suddenly saw him carrying this big weight toward me, something unbearably heavy that he was going to put right in my lap."

I don't say anything. He draws himself a glass of water, clears his throat, coughs, sniffs, sighs, puts the glass, then his head, on the counter. He says, "Ma, I could sleep for six days."

"So take a nap."

"Okay." And he weaves out, as if drained of strength. I

begin frosting the cake, green, because there's nothing Diane likes better than a chocolate cake with green icing. As I put the cake in the refrigerator, the noise of the lawnmower dies, and a second or so later, Joe throws back the screen door. I think of what I might say—I need to go to the bathroom, the store, K-mart, next door, anywhere, right now. Let me evade the coming confidences. It is a physical urge, a shrinking—not from Joe himself but from what I will become in the next fifteen minutes—reassuring, objective, soothing, fat somehow. It is a way I have always been with Joe more than the others. Each of them has approached me with a different request—Ellen's has always been, "What is true?" and to the best of my ability I have always been relieved to tell her. Daniel's has always been, "Is it okay if I do this?" and I have always been able to say "yes" or "no." And his response has always been that he was going to do it anyway. Annie's every look and gesture says, "Can you see me yet?" and so she is flamboyant and prickly and hilariously funny. Michael has had the simplest request, directed only at me, and that has been, "Do you love me best?" and my answer, directed only at him, has been, "I can't." We know where we stand.

But Joe, Joe's question is directed everywhere, and it is unanswerable. It is, "Am I okay? Tell me that I am just okay, and that is enough for me." He is okay. He is smart and thoughtful and nice-looking. He is doing well in a prestigious program at a good school. When he wants a date or a girlfriend, he can get one. "You are okay," I say. "You have to say that, you're my mom," he says, or, I imagine, "you're my girlfriend, you're my major adviser, you're my friend." Nothing can induce him to believe that he is okay. How did I overlook him when he was a baby? I remember praising, hugging, paying attention, taking delight. Were there simply too many? But we thought we were doing them a favor, giving them lots of others besides ourselves

to learn from and get close to. Pat had six brothers and
sisters, and spoke rapturously of the family fun-fair, of the
delight he took in listening to his mother address him as
"Tim-Jackie-Joe-Jimmy-PATRICK!", as if he shared in all the
qualities that he adored in his older brothers. I thought my
aunts and uncles, who spoke fondly of their adventures on
the farm as children, had had a much more exciting time
than I was having by myself. Old justifications. Five kids
in five years is a lot of kids. Nobody would approve today.
In 1963, when Ellen pushed a grocery cart with one twin
in it and I pushed the other and Daniel and Annie trailed
behind, everyone smiled at us. Fifty 1963 dollars handed
over at the checkout stand? A figure to be proud of.

Joe says, "There's nothing there. We don't think alike
anymore. I am on my own now."

"You seem to be getting along fine, honey."

"But we thought alike. We thought the same thoughts.
We both always used to say that. You know that character
on 'Sesame Street,' the two-headed Russian guy who's always arguing with himself?"

"Joe—"

"That was us. We used to laugh like hell at that, and run
around the TV room shouting in mock Russian."

"Joe, you're grown men. Do you want to be like those
twins who dress alike and cultivate their twinship forever?
I know you don't!"

"You don't want us to, Dad doesn't want us to, Michael
doesn't want to, but I DO!"

"Honey—"

"Isn't that awful? I'm a man! How can I say that? Just to
say it fills me with self-loathing. I wish we were girls or
something. I know some girl twins. None of this comes up
with them. Separate identities is just one option with them.
With us it's the only option."

"But it's not healthy for any set—"

"How do you know that? How does anybody know that who isn't one? Ma—"

"What?"

"Tell me this isn't any big deal."

"I don't know if it's a big deal. In the first place, Michael couldn't possibly be himself right now, and I think you're putting a lot of pressure on him—"

"That's true." He caves in instantly, as always, to any criticism. "After Louise broke up with me, I longed for him so much. I thought, I can't have her, but I'll always have him. It's fucked. Why do I care? You're right. Men have to be by themselves."

"There's something to be said for being by yourself."

"Well, I know you think that. Don't you remember once, when I was about four, I followed you into the bathroom and you said, 'Joe, I like to be by myself, don't you understand?' and I said, 'No,' and I didn't. I never did."

"Look," I say. "Michael's asleep and we don't have to be at Ellen's until six. Remember when we went to that exhibition downtown and we said we'd like to go back and spend more time? This is the last weekend. Let's do that. Let's get out of the house."

"No, Mom! That's not the point! Just forget it!" He is out of the room before I can say another thing.

When we pull up at Ellen's, Jerry is on a bike in the street, doing figure eights with no hands. Diane and Tracy are watching him. He's good. Sometimes he gives the bike a calculated wobble, as if he is going to fall over, and the girls scream. They run over when they see us, and I hand Diane the cake. I see her stick her tongue out and lick the frosting. She sees me see her. We smile. Ellen comes out of the front door, carrying a pitcher of water. She says, "Hey! You're here!" She puts down the pitcher next to the pots of geraniums on the porch, and comes over to kiss us. Her glance travels toward Jerry and away without falling on him.

After an afternoon of silence, Joe and Michael and I spoke politely to one another in the car. Gingerly. Now Tracy's eyes flick from her mother to her father and back again; then Ellen says, without actually looking at Jerry, who has stopped his bike and put his feet on the pavement, "Dinner at six-thirty, okay?"

"Okay," says Jerry.

"Come on in, Mom." For us she has a smile. "I made some wine coolers, but Diane said I had to offer Kool-Aid, too, so I have lime Kool-Aid."

We pause in the living room, looking for places to sit down, but she calls from the kitchen, "Come in here, where I can see you."

"Kool-Aid for me," says Joe.

She puts a wine cooler in front of me, and pauses in front of Michael with her hands on her hips. "Got any beer?" he says.

"Budweiser."

"I'll take it." Diane comes in the back door with the cake. It looks okay, but I wonder what she has been doing with it for the last five minutes. I say, "Sweetie, you'd better put that in the refrigerator so the icing doesn't drip off."

"Can Jennifer come over and have some after her dinner?"

"Jennifer was here for thirty-six straight hours, darling. Maybe we should give her a rest."

"She doesn't want a rest."

"Maybe I want a rest."

"Oh, Mom!" Diane's voice rises to a whine. Ellen rolls her eyes, and says, "All right, all right. Go out now, okay? She can come back at seven-thirty."

"Seven o'clock."

"Seven-fifteen. Give us a chance to eat, for God's sake."

Diane runs out.

"This one's right up your alley, Joe," says Ellen.

"What's her field?"

"She seems like a generalist to me. At breakfast this morning, she memorized where everyone was sitting; then, at lunch, she made detailed inquiries about why we weren't sitting in the same chairs, then about where I got the chairs and why they don't match." She laughs, sobers up. "I shouldn't make fun of her, but it's such a temptation."

"Oh," says Joe, "they need that. It tempers their sense of difference from the others."

Ellen loves to toss off vignettes. If someone is boring, and has literally never done anything worth repeating, Ellen will make something up about him: "Don't you wonder about Ray Bradley, Mom? He seems so bland. Just the sort of person to be a terrible dope addict—shoots it right into the eyeball now, after collapsing every vein in his body." Every time Joe brings up one of his geniuses, Ellen teases him for the envy she can hear in his voice: "And who was Kafka? Just another guy who let women take care of him. 'Fritzi,' she says, 'this way. This way into the post office.'" Joe likes it—his basic assumptions are unmoved—he laughs, he envisions his geniuses with faces and behaviors.

She should have gone to medical school or law school. I think we all assumed she would, especially Jerry, who once went into her file and Xeroxed all her recommendations: "Best student I ever had," "Brilliant mind," "First-rate intelligence, but, more than that, consuming curiosity, terrific imagination," "A talent for synthesizing information that amounts to genius." She told all her professors that she had her eye on some kind of professional training, and got their recommendations, but she never sent her file anywhere, never even made an application. She married Jerry, who was thirty-seven by then, and had Diane at once, then Tracy. She had excuses that almost amounted to reasons: Jerry was too old to wait long for kids, she hadn't decided what sort

of career she wanted, no money for school with the bookstore and all. "I'm just lazy," was what she finally said, and
that has been her position for years. Jerry says, "It's a
crime."

They had this argument in front of me once—it's more
teasing now than anything else—"It's not a crime. It isn't
even a misdemeanor. I can do what I want."

"You're wasting your gift."

"I don't think it's of much value, frankly. Highly over-
rated. Full many a flower is born to blush unseen, and waste
its sweetness on the desert air, you know."

"That's in England. You can't do that in America." And
these arguments always end in a shrug. My approach was
different—children can't stand that much attention, I said,
especially when there are only two of them. They need
to go unwatched in order to develop their inner lives. A
shrug. "I work in the bookstore, Mother. That's very time-
consuming." I know. What is there to say? Joe, I think,
would like to trade recommendations. His always say,
"Kinsella is one of my brighter students in recent years,"
and Joe always says, "Thank God all the geniuses are in
engineering. If they were around, I wouldn't be noticed
at all."

Sometimes I relish a small sense of privilege, sitting
around, listening to Ellen's tales rise into the air and vanish
like soap bubbles, and I remember that Pat's conversations
were like that, and I feel a little twinge of loss. Ellen says,
exasperated, to Jerry and to me, "Isn't it all right just to
live and die? Why does there have to be a record?" In the
last eight years, her refusal to make something of herself
has hardened into a position. I wonder why I care. Maybe
there is a lingering pride, like the pride I had of Michael
and Joe—the pride of producing a phenomenon. I would
like the opus to be on display a little.

When I was married to Pat, I got to be intransigently and

loudly unambitious. Never impressed, that was me. Lee Salk came to give a lecture, and Pat showed him around. I couldn't have cared less. Some Nobel laureate in medicine, from England, actually came to our house for dinner. I made myself forget his name. I met Pat and this man at the door in my bedroom slippers. I had become my uncles, asking silently, "But can he castrate a hog? Build a fence? Get the cows into the barn during a blizzard?" I looked at them all with Viking skepticism. If when these great men appeared I could have had my aunts and uncles around me, talking scours and winter wheat, mud on their boots and tools in the pockets of their overalls, sometimes lapsing into the half-English, half-Norwegian dialect that they spoke among themselves when outsiders were around, I would have. And when the teachers were dazzled with Ellen in grammar school, I always diminished it. So maybe I short-circuited my own phenomenon. I wouldn't do it now. Now I know that she is rare and valuable, but she refuses to know it.

She still sucks up information. She sits by the cash register at the bookstore on a tall stool, reading. And the bookstore has a little sign above the clock that says, "Please read the books. Don't just break the bindings." Now she leans back and drains her wine cooler and a shiver passes through her. Jerry crosses the deck outside the screen door and her glance shoots toward him and away. I say, "The lawnmower's fixed. The grass is cut."

"You going to have it baled? You can get three dollars a bale these days."

"Let's do that," Joe says. "Let's farm Mom's yard. Let's run hogs and turkeys between the house and the garage."

Michael smiles a tired smile, which Joe is looking for out of the corner of his eye. When it comes, Joe himself smiles. When Joe turns toward me, I look at the tablecloth. Yes, I am offended with him. He doesn't have to parade his every feeling. Now he gets up and lifts the lids on the stove, then opens the oven. A sharp, spicy, delicious smell billows toward me, full of cumin and pepper. Joe bends down and puts his head farther into the oven. "Mmmm," he says, "let's eat."

"Cholesterol special," says Ellen. "Cheese enchiladas with sour cream. I made guacamole, too, and beans and rice." She leans toward Michael, pokes him in the stomach. "This is for you, bub. We might keel over at the table, but you'll put on ten pounds."

Michael says, "Hey, Joe, remember that girl you knew in college who gained twenty pounds one semester, but she was so rail-thin no one could figure out where she put it, so one day she walked into the lounge after dinner, when I was visiting you, and she lifted up her dress and let her stomach out, just to show everyone, and it was like she had swallowed a bowling ball?"

"LeeAnn Clapper. I always wanted to date her."

After dinner Jerry corners me in the kitchen and says in a low voice, "Has Ellen talked to you?"

I am carrying dishes. I put them down. "What about?"

"Oh, well, a few threats passed this afternoon."

"Which direction?"

"Both."

"Going to be carried out?"

"Not mine. I'm not sure about hers."

"Which threat?"

"The big one."

"Impossible," I say.

"It always has seemed impossible with Ellen, but she's drawn to it. She brings it up. You know what Updike says."

"What?"

"If it comes up, then it will happen."

I put my hands on my hips and say, "It's not a rowboat

heading toward Niagara Falls, Jerry. If there's something you're arguing about, you can get help to settle it."

"I didn't before. Did you?"

"Did you want to before? I didn't."

"I don't know what it is, exactly. We never argue about money or kids. We've even stopped arguing about sex. We just argue about what we suspect the other one is thinking about us. It doesn't even have to do with love, especially. She accuses me of being angry at her for no reason; then I accuse her of not liking the way I spend my time, learning to fly and everything; and then we're just screaming! And I think, Yes, I am angry a lot of the time, and I do get into these pointless obsessions that cost money and won't head anywhere like a career or anything, and, yes, she is judgmental and hyperrational and expects everything everyone does to be orderly and reasonable. And then I see us as these ranting neurotics, mismatched except in the scope of our misconceptions. And THEN I go up to the bathroom and stare into the mirror and think that I am forty-six and I was never very good-looking to begin with, and maybe what she's really telling me is that she's gotten attracted to another man, some thirty-year-old kid whose body is absolutely in its prime."

I look around Jerry, and there is Ellen, bright-eyed. She says, "Confiding in Mom again, huh? Go ahead. I don't care. Ready for coffee? I don't have time for another man."

I smile.

"What are you smiling about?" says Ellen.

"Nothing."

"Yes you are. You absolutely grinned. I mean, it wasn't merry, but it was a grin."

"Probably a wince. Nothing."

She looks at me suspiciously, but doesn't press me. I begin to rinse dishes. This child, Jennifer, comes through the swinging door and says, "May I have another piece of cake,

Ellen?" Then, to me, "Rachel, did you make the frosting green on purpose?"

"Yes."

"Why?"

"Because Diane likes that color."

"But—" says Jennifer. Ellen hands her a plate with a piece of cake on it and says, "Go out and play now, Jennifer."

"May I take the plate and the fork outside?"

"Yes."

"Where do you want me to put them when I bring them in?"

"In the sink will be fine."

"What if there are crumbs on the plate?"

"That's okay. Go OUT, Jennifer."

"Okay." She goes out, but not without a long stare at everything in the room, including me.

Ellen says, "I speak to her in tones I would never use to anyone else. I'm sure everyone does. Sort of exasperated and overly direct. She's only seven. How did she get this way so fast? Anyway, Diane loves her, loves the way she just plants her feet wide apart in the middle of the room and addresses all adults by their first names, even the teachers at school." Ellen throws her head back and laughs at the thought. Then, "Okay, Mother," she says, "why did you grin?"

"I didn't mean to."

"Yes, you meant to hide what you were thinking, just like you always do."

"I say what I think."

"You are honest. But you aren't open. So tell me."

"I was just reminded of something."

"What?"

"Why are you pressing me? It doesn't have anything to do with you and Jerry."

"All the more reason for you to tell me."

"Ellen!"

"Go ahead and get mad. It doesn't scare me, and I want to know, and I am going to nag you for days until you tell me."

"It's something I haven't thought about in a long time that I just happened to think about. No big deal."

"Now you sound like Joe. Every time Joe says that, that means it's a really big deal. I've got my eye on you, Mother." She means it. She carries the coffeepot through the swinging door.

When she comes back into the kitchen, where I have almost finished the dishes, she says, "You want to know what I think we were arguing about?"

"What?"

"I mean, apart from the perennial question of whether women have sex drive, the way Jerry always wants me out of the house. I mean, I admit that I am crabby today. But as soon as I asked him to hand me the bread this morning, he said I should go out somewhere. To the Y for a sauna, or out to breakfast. It's like he's afraid I'm going to do damage or something. It's just a bad mood, it's not a homicidal rage. Except that there he is, glancing at me and shushing the kids and muffling the rustle of the newspaper, and pretty soon it is a homicidal rage! I don't WANT to go out. I HATE to go out. I like to be right here, or else maybe in the dining room. Why doesn't he understand that about me? It's him that wants to go out, and fly planes solo and ride his bike to Bloomington."

"You're just telling me, aren't you? You're not expecting me to make any reply?"

"No. No, I'm not. It's over, anyway. Come have coffee." She takes the pot and goes out through the swinging door.

Of course I was thinking of Ed, the way I fit him in in spite of everything. Who is the busiest person in the world, busier than a woman with five children and a kitchen being remodeled? Had I been that person, even then I would have fit him in.

In the dining room, Jerry and Michael are talking about India and Joe is sitting on the floor by the door to the living room, going through some of the stacks of books. Jerry keeps saying, "Are you kidding me?" and his continuing incredulity seems to warm Michael up. He says, "No, really. We got to about fourteen thousand feet, and it was nothing. I mean, imagine it. You're three or four thousand feet higher than you would be in the Tetons, say, and all around you there are still peaks as high above you as if you were standing, not at the base of the Tetons, but at sea level. It's not like anything you've ever seen or felt. I mean, the world is so much bigger than you think it's going to be."

Jerry, leaning forward on his elbows, says, "Wow. Did you take any pictures?"

"Well, it was too big to take pictures. I didn't have good equipment, not even a wide-angle lens, and it was fucking cold, too. So I thought, Shit, I'm never going to forget this anyway."

"I can't tell you how envious I feel right this minute."

Me, too.

Michael tips back his chair and looks at the ceiling, then says to Jerry, "I wonder if you should. I mean, yeah, I saw it, and it was astonishing and unforgettable, just like the whole trip. But I feel too spread out now, like I've been rolled out with a rolling pin and I can't gather myself in to focus on anything. Yeah, that's it. I've just figured it out. I want to go everywhere now—Japan, New Zealand, Antarctica, for God's sake—but when you go to those places, you're just this little pinpoint sort of pushing through them, and when you visualize them in your mind, it's like you're a balloon, inflating and thinning out so you can hold it all. Everything is frustrating. You can't be there completely enough when you're there, and when you've understood sort of what it's like to be there, you aren't there any more. I think humans are genetically programmed to stay in one place all their lives. I think one place is exactly what you can understand."

Ellen says, "Then why is the history of mankind the history of travel? It seems to me that humans organize their societies in two ways—either as nomadic ones, where everyone walks thousands of miles in his lifetime, or as settlements that everyone flees and then returns to. I think humans are genetically programmed to go. Simply to go until the batteries are dead."

"It's the eyes," says Joe from his corner. "Your eyes make you think that you are somewhere where you really aren't. I mean, think about it. A man is walking down the stairs. At the bottom is the front door. He sees the front door, and his car outside, and because he sees them, in his mind he is already there, he has already walked down the stairs, even though he is still walking down them. A piece of carpet is loose. His foot, which is exactly where it is in time and space, catches on the carpet and he falls down the stairs and breaks his neck. He has been fatally deceived by the illusion that your eyes always cast over you, which is that THERE is more important than HERE, and, since time and space are the same thing, the future is more important than now."

Jerry says, "I would still like to see it."

Me, too.

I say, "Would you prefer not to have seen it?" Michael looks at me for a long time—not at me, really, but at his own thought. We all look at him, waiting. He says, "I would prefer not to be shaped by experiences. I would like to just have them, not to incorporate them." He sighs.

"You'd like to be a computer, then," says Joe.

It turns out that Jennifer spends the night, although she spent the night last night. When Ellen calls her mother, the woman says, "Oh, fine."

And now it is after nine. We are sitting on the back deck. Joe and Michael, between whom I can still see a stiffness, and Jerry and Ellen, ditto, are drinking beer. I am having another glass of wine, and no one has spoken for about five minutes. There is no light except the ambient light of the city spread out above us. I can see their figures, rather bluish, distributed around me, and hear their movements. Ellen says, idly, "Okay, Mom, why did you grin in the kitchen?"

I admit I am startled. This conversation seems more appropriate to the kitchen, to just Ellen and myself. Except, of course, that she doesn't know what I was grimacing about, and she thinks this is a way to twit me, maybe, something she likes to do. I can't say I don't know. I can say something general—about desire, maybe, about how if a person wants something enough there is always room for it. She knows I think desire is the only motivation. Or I could make up a story about someone at work, some woman with a job and a bunch of kids and a husband and a lover on the side. She goes without lunch, she goes without noontime aerobics, she picks up her kids half an hour later at the day-care center. She is rigidly alert, the way I was. I could make her live, make them laugh at her, the way Joe and Michael laughed at the Shoe Man. She's dressed a little better every day than she used to be, wearing a little more makeup, so focused and attentive that her work is not only always done, her desk is always neat. She straightens it compulsively, doesn't she? A new life is coursing through her unlike any previous life—this time she is married, and what she feels is compounded equally of terror and desire. I could say she knows what I know but didn't know twenty years ago, that both the terror and the desire will be fulfilled, and equally. This woman is suddenly so real to me that thinking of her here in the dark has an odd effect. I think, why not? Why not tell them? They are grown up now, have had passions of their own. I've never told anyone what it was like with Ed, and what happened to it. Ellen is right. Though honest, I have also always been secretive. Or, no, I have not always been secretive. I used to be reserved, and then, twenty years ago, I became secretive.

Silhouetted against the silver of the house, Joe tips up his beer and takes the last drops. All summer he has been after me to fill in blanks for him, but only certain blanks. He does think that I am sexless, in that motherish way, and he dismisses me for it, the way men always dismiss women whom they don't imagine to be objects of desire. Well, I have let him, haven't I? Pat remarried a beautiful young woman, produced more young children in his forties. But my great passion was buying a house, and I acted as if Simon were primarily a handyman and never kissed him in front of the children. And Ellen. Our comfort together, our sense of kinship, is made up of children, cooking, gossip about the bookstore and the office, but never this. I know she assumes that our parting was Pat's fault. I say, in a voice as idle as Ellen's, "My experience is that you make room for anything you want, if you want it enough. Even an inconvenient man."

Ellen's head turns, and she says, "Yeah?" but the men do not move. Her eyes are dark, and I can't tell if they say "Go on" or if they say "Don't." I go on. I say, "I made room for Ed."

Joe says, "Who was Ed? I don't remember an Ed."

"Ed was the third point of the triangle that ended my marriage with your father. He lived down the road, in the old farmhouse that had been on the property before it was subdivided."

"In the country?" says Joe. He speaks of the country, as always, in golden, longing tones.

"Yes. I met him because he had an old horse that he used

to ride bareback up and down the lane. I used to ride bare-back in Nebraska, so once we got to talking about horses. He was a writer, though. Edward Stackhouse."

Ellen says, "I've heard of him."

"Mmm," I say. "It was an old horse, very swaybacked. Came with the farmhouse. He used to stop when Michael and Joe and I were walking down the lane, and put Michael up in front of him. Joe didn't want to, ever."

Joe says, "Was it a white horse?"

"Very light dappled gray, yes. Ed used to laugh at everything I said. He would stop, and I would stop what I was doing, and we would talk. Then we talked longer. His eyes were a strange color, kind of a Federal blue. He'd been everywhere, even though he was still in his twenties. His wife had left him, so I think we made a lovely picture for him, twins, remodeling, lawns and gardens, dinner at seven, very Kennedyesque. He made a lovely picture, too. Austere, solitary, artistic. He'd worked for some of Kennedy's speechwriters, and now he was working on some sort of White House book. I couldn't stay away from him."

At this, there is an assortment of little noises—a laugh from Michael, a grunt from Joe. From Ellen, a little ex-halation, sharp but nearly inaudible. As I speak, I remember more. Nothing can stop me now.

"All he ever had in the house was coffee. I didn't drink coffee before or after that, but I always did with him. He made it for me, very creamy and sweet."

"Where were we?" says Michael.

"At first you were always with me, but then the summer came, and your father put the older kids in day camp and you into nursery school three mornings a week. I was never really sure he would be glad to see me if I came without you, so, even when we were sleeping together and our meetings were regular, I would make up some little excuse for coming down the lane. That part was crazy."

"That part?" says Ellen.

"Well, yes. I mean, I knew I was expected, but even so I always had to bring something, some flowers or a loaf of bread, like a hostess gift, and then, when we began to undress one another, I always had to pretend to myself that I hadn't been thinking of that, or that this body that was appearing out of my clothes was a big surprise to me."

"Sounds like love, Ma," says Michael.

"I don't know. It wasn't excitement like that. It felt most like some fixed, inconsolable longing. It was constant, even when I was at his place. I would go over there, and it would stop the moment I saw him, but only that moment. After that there was so much that he was holding back from me that I was as filled with longing when I was with him as when I wasn't. After we made love, he would sleep and I would lie there wondering what you kids were doing at camp and nursery school."

Joe says, "Sounds upbeat, Ma. Sounds life-affirming." His voice is subdued.

"Did Daddy have the place under surveillance?" says Ellen. "Were you being followed by two German men in a black van?"

"He didn't suspect until I told him. Maybe that was the most important thing about it."

"What did you tell him?"

"That I was seeing Ed and I didn't want to stop. But I did stop. The relationship didn't outlast the marriage."

Michael says, "Why did you tell him?"

"Well, the whole affair was a terrible strain, for one thing." They are staring at me, which makes this explanation seem trivial. I suppose all the explanations I've considered over the past twenty years seem trivial, in light of the consequences. I begin the self-justification—"I didn't know what—I thought—" but I can't bear it. I look from one to another.

Finally, I say, "I wanted him to know I wasn't his." Such a little thing, with them looking at me like this.

After a moment Jerry says, "So this Ed, what happened to him?"

"About a week after Pat took everyone to England, he said he wouldn't see me or speak to me again. He was a very absolute sort of person. Sometimes I saw him around, but he kept to his word. He never spoke to me again."

"Why?"

"I wrote and asked him that a couple of times. He didn't answer. I thought then that he was just cruel, or that he hated me. I couldn't explain it any other way. After that I thought that he must have been afraid of me and of what he'd done."

Michael says, "How long did it take you to get over it?"

"I stopped loving Ed about a year later. Really stopped. Didn't even recognize him at Kroger's. But I don't think I ever got over it. Every time I ever got interested in anyone after that, I felt such conflicting feelings of desire and defeat that it was too frightening. Even with Simon. I could have gotten closer to Simon, but I couldn't. I just couldn't let go beyond a certain point without wanting to kill myself."

"Wanting to kill yourself?" Michael seems to assert some kind of primacy here, as if all of this is more his business than the others'. We trade a glance, and I am not sure what I see there, but it isn't surprise. I say, "It wasn't sadness, actually. It was the sense of having been drawn in and drawn in, encouraged to have trust, to open up. Ed loved to talk, for me to talk. That's mostly what we did. And then it was suddenly gone. It was unaccountable. It was the mystery that made me want to kill myself, not exactly loss. That feeling of opening up got awfully entwined with the feeling of mysterious danger. But look at it—I let myself go, and then I got punished for it. By Ed, and by your father, too.

And I thought I deserved it. And I thought I might never see you all again. So, no, I never got over it. I never let go again, because I never wanted to want to kill myself again." I look at Michael, but he is looking across the yard. I say, after a moment, "I don't think I loved Ed the most. But it's not necessarily the ones you love the most that have the most effect on you."

"So," says Ellen, "who did you love the most?"

"Oh, your father, I suppose."

Now Ellen looks at me again, and says, "Come on, Mother, how could you?"

I say, "Well, it's not because he was the first or anything, or even because I spent the most time with him. He was exciting. Besides, you're not asking me to compare the feelings I have about him now with feelings I had about others then. You're asking me to compare one delusion with another." We all chuckle awkwardly. There is another long silence. I don't know how the story has affected them, but having told it makes me hollow with fear. It is the way that I have contained it all these years that has given me strength, and now it seems to me that I have risked that. And then Ellen says, "I've got a story, too. You want to hear my story?"

Jerry, on the chaise longue, sits up and looks at us. He says, "Does this include a lover?"

"No," says Ellen. "It includes Daddy, and you've heard it before, so why don't you bring out some more beers?" Jerry gets up. Ellen is looking at me, and when Jerry turns on the kitchen light, I can see her face. Her look is neither confiding nor meditative, but calmly vengeful. Now it is my turn to think, Don't, to realize that what she meant when she said, "How could you?" was how dare I say I loved Pat the most after all these years, after the abandonment, after the battles and the enmity. She meant, how could

I betray her loyalty to me at this late date. Something she is about to say will be my punishment, and I shrink from hearing it, but I am eager, too.

Michael says, "What's your story?"

Ellen turns to him. "Do you remember Jenny? She was a Dutch girl, about twenty-five, that Daddy brought back with him to the States. She lived with us for about three months and then left?"

"Blonde?" says Michael.

"Yes. Very short. Not much taller than I was at eleven."

Michael shrugs.

"Evil stepmother?" says Joe.

"Oh, no," says Ellen. "She was nice enough. She was just a kid. She was always baking cookies and eating them. She couldn't speak very good English, but she would bake these cookies, and then she and Daniel and I would sit at the kitchen table and just eat them and smile at one another. I think she felt sorry for us, because she knew she could leave Daddy but we couldn't."

"So?" says Joe.

Ellen sits back and looks out over the yard. "One day when we were in England, I got up real early and came down into the kitchen, and Daddy was sitting there all dressed up in a suit, drinking a cup of coffee. It was still dark, so it must have been winter. I asked him why he was all dressed up, and he said that he had to rush over to Amsterdam to get Jenny, did I remember Jenny, and bring her back to take care of us, would I like that? Well, I didn't know, but I knew Holland was across the ocean and farther away than a single day's trip, so I asked if we were going along, and he said no, Mrs. Frith, the daily woman, was going to look after us during the day. And I said, 'Well, who's going to look after us at night?' and he said, 'It will only be one night, and this is England, and you are nearly eleven, and Daniel is a big boy, and so I think, if you lock

the doors and draw the curtains, everything will be fine.'
Pretty soon he finished his coffee and got up and gave me
a kiss and left, and I don't know what he was thinking.
What if I hadn't gotten up so early? What if I had just missed
him completely?"

"He wasn't thinking," says Joe. "He was following his
dick to Holland. That's what Father used to do."

"Anyway," Ellen continues, "pretty soon Annie got up,
and I got her dressed and then Daniel and you guys, and I
thought that Mrs. Frith would come to take us to our school.
We were all ready, dressed and fed, and we sort of sat by
the door, waiting, for a long time. But Mrs. Frith didn't
get there until about noon, and so by that time everyone
was doing other things, and I didn't say anything to her
about it. She was a very cheery woman, Mrs. Frith, but
maybe she drank or thought we were odd because we were
Americans, because she never asked anything about it, and
at one point I said, 'Did my father say he was going on a
trip?' and she said, 'Why no, luv,' and so I just didn't say
another word. She left about five.

"Well, she had made us something to eat—that was one
thing she did when she came—and at six o'clock I dished
it up, exactly at six o'clock, because Daddy always liked
that kind of precision and I had this sense that if I did everything right he would get back quicker—early enough the
next day to take us to school. The funny thing was that no
one asked where he was, at least none of the younger kids.
But Michael and Joe fought like crazy, yelling and pushing
each other and crying, from after dinner until about nine-
thirty, when I decided it was bedtime. I did just what Daddy
said—I pulled the curtains and locked the door and refused
to be afraid. Daniel started reading through his entire comic-
book collection that he'd brought with him from the States,
for about the tenth time, and Annie kept looking at me, but
she didn't say much and I didn't volunteer anything.

"The next day I let everybody sleep late, but I was looking for him from about dawn. Mrs. Frith came and we were all still in our pyjamas, but she didn't say anything. She did ask where Daddy was, and I said that he had gone to the hospital very early, and left word that we didn't have to go to school. I was just very embarrassed that he hadn't come back. She made us put on our clothes, though. By Friday she was more suspicious, but I made up this long story about how he was coming home right after work to take us to Ireland for a week, and I even said that she could call him at the hospital and ask him if she liked, but I knew she wouldn't because she was very suspicious of the telephone and hated to call anyone up, especially Daddy, who hated to hear from anyone when he was at work.

"Well, I remember that on Friday I became convinced that he wasn't coming back, and that I was going to have to figure out a way to take care of everyone and pay for everything—Mrs. Frith, for one. I thought all day about how she got paid on Monday, and that when Monday rolled around I wasn't going to have anything to pay her, much less pay the rent or buy food, and all Friday I was kind of rigid with fear. Michael and Joe were terrible again—fighting and running around and I thought really hurting each other—and Daniel kept saying that everybody had to get outside and go to the park. Annie was very subdued, for which I was grateful, but I was afraid that she would start crying.

"Finally, on Saturday, I let Daniel convince me to go to the park, and so we put on our clothes very neatly, so that no one would know that we didn't have any parents, and we started walking in a line to the park. I held Annie's hand, and Daniel had Michael and Joe, one on each side. It was incredibly far, and lots of people were out shopping, and at one point Daniel and Michael ran up and said that Joe had broken away and disappeared, and he really was gone, for about three minutes I couldn't see him anywhere, and I looked at Annie, and she was just taking it all in, sort of appalled. Then Joe appeared, he was looking at a store window, and we ran over and grabbed him. So Daniel said that we shouldn't go to the park, it was too far, and he couldn't handle Michael and Joe both, so we turned around and went home and ate biscuits.

"On Sunday I decided that I was going to empty the trash, and I was carrying the basket down the stairs of the apartment building when this woman came up to me that I'd seen in the lift once or twice, and she said, 'You children are making a great deal of noise.' So I apologized, and she said, 'Your father should take you to the park and give the other residents some peace. Your father is that tall man, isn't he?' And then she paused and stared at me, and said, 'I haven't seen your father for days.' And I said, just as cool as you please, 'Well, really, he went to Holland and I don't believe he's coming back.' And I walked away."

She pauses, and there are things I could say, but I don't know what they are. Where was I? Getting up in my barren apartment, walking into my clothes and out the door, writing Pat letters every day, begging him to bring home the children. By the end of winter he still hadn't replied the first time.

"Monday morning she showed up at the door with a lady in a suit, who walked around the apartment and looked in the cupboards and the refrigerator and asked me some questions. I mean, I wasn't an idiot. I had read *Oliver Twist* by that time, and I recognized a Mr. Bumble the Beadle when I saw her. I knew the boys would be in one building and Annie and I would be in another, and that our dolls and books would be taken away from us, and eventually we would be farmed out to gangs of street thieves." She laughs suddenly, but she is the only one who does. "So all that day I cleaned, and made Daniel clean, too. In fact, we locked

Michael and Joe in their room for five hours so that we could get the place looking decent, in case that would persuade the authorities that we could take care of ourselves. I pulled all the food in the cupboards out and rearranged it so it would look like more than it was.

"About noon the next day, this car pulls up outside with 'South Kensington Christian Children's Home' written on the side, and I got Daniel and we put a chair in front of the door and ran into one of the bedrooms and hid. We told Annie and Michael and Joe that some people were coming to take us away—which was the literal truth, wasn't it?—and made them be quiet, and we just sat there. There was a knock on the door, then silence, then another knock on the door, and then a key in the lock! And I couldn't believe they had a key. I really thought we were doomed. So I crawl to the bedroom door and open it a crack, and Michael and Joe wiggle under the bed, and I see the front door open against the chair, and then it slams open and the chair falls out of the way, and there's Daddy, with Mrs. Beadle behind him, and is he ever in a rage, yelling about state interference in family life, and socialized medicine and entrepreneurship, one of those trains of thought association Daddy goes into. Something about the atrophy of private initiative and the moribund path of English medical research. I mean, he walked in like he always does, opening windows for fresh air, calling out for us, taking off his tie all at the same time, and what were they going to do? What did I want him to do? I was thrilled to see him."

"I'm sure," says Joe, "that he thinks he was only gone for a night or two. I'm sure he thought it then. I mean, remember how he used to smack us and then say that we had just run into his fist?"

"Mmm," says Michael.

And I don't say anything. Can she really remember so much detail? But that doesn't matter, anyway, does it? I don't ask if that ten-year-old ever thought of her mother, was ever tempted to call me across the ocean on the phone. There is a perfect logic in her story, the practical acceptance of losing first one parent, then the other, of being handed a set of impossible tasks. It is fairy tale logic, the one sort of logic a ten-year-old understands perfectly. I don't say, "Incredible! Unbelievable!" although I would never have thought it possible for Pat to leave them alone for six days in London. I do believe. I believe because Joe and Michael are so matter-of-fact. I believe, in fact, because Ellen's story is so specific. I believe because this supplies a large, perfectly fitting piece in the puzzle of her adult life, the piece with the eyes on it, you might say, the eyes that keep a careful lookout for Diane and Tracy and Jerry and me. Vigilance is her full-time job. I believe because, although I am shocked, I am not surprised. Pat was always unrestrained, sudden, passionate, single-minded. The children could as easily be out of his focus as in it. And I am not surprised because my deepest fear is realized. The three-year-old stepping onto the wrong elevator, the wrong train, losing grip of your hand just for the moment when the doors slam shut. Watching the crowded train shoot off toward Saint Louis, Chicago, San Francisco. The six-year-old, even the ten-year-old, lost in the crowd, and the crowd parts and she has vanished. It is a fear greater than the fear of their deaths. An eagle dives down and sweeps the child from your arms, the water rises and wrenches her away. The lost, living child, bobbing on the waves of its own resourcefulness. I am punished indeed. The others go on talking, unsurprised by their father. I can't speak. Ellen casts me a couple of looks, then says, "I think I'll check on the girls, just to see if they're sleeping yet." She knows she has amply repaid me for my candor, but her expression is ruthless. I suspect there won't be much comfort here for a while. Sometime later we go home.

Joe drives, Michael rides in front, I sit deep in the back seat, out of the glare of passing streetlights. They talk about Pat, and I listen. Joe says, "Do you think Jenny was the one with the breasts? Remember that, when we were all sitting around the breakfast table, and he started kissing that girl, and then he took off her blouse and kissed her breasts, with us sitting right there?"

"And you dumped your oatmeal on his pants?" They laugh. Michael says, "That was later, I think. We were at least seven for that. I can't remember if that was when you were living with us or just visiting."

"Well, it all sort of melts together in a merciful blur, thank God."

They drive in silence.

Michael says, soberly, "Well, he was the worst to Daniel, that's for sure."

"Remember that time I went to the Grand Canyon with you? How long was that for, a month? And everything that went wrong he blamed on Daniel. I mean, even when he had some kind of fight with Tatty, the next morning he said over breakfast that Daniel had talked in his sleep and wakened her up, and that the real problem was that she couldn't stand to be with Daniel and she took it out on Daddy, and why was Daniel so disagreeable and hard to get along with, was he intent on breaking up Daddy's second marriage, too? I remember that distinctly."

"I remember thinking, So that's what happened with Mom, Daniel did it."

"Me, too."

"Daniel, too, I'll bet." They sigh. But their tones are matter-of-fact, as if they have plowed this ground before. And another thing is true—they have forgotten about me in that twinlike way.

What they say creates a vast and complicated but vividly articulated new object in my mind, the history of my chil-

dren in my absence, at the mercy of their father. Didn't I
know he was like this, unrestrained and blind to the potential
consequences of his own actions? Before we got married,
he would make love to me anywhere—in the kitchen,
against the refrigerator, with the possibility that his room-
mate would walk in at any time, often in his car, sometimes
right beside the highway, where he had pulled over in the
middle of the trip, more than once on the floor of his lab,
with the door unlocked. He was passionate. I didn't protest.
I thought I was irresistible. After we had children, I said
over and over, always laughing, "Come on. People don't
make love when the children are around." I still thought I
was irresistible, though. Angry, his language was always
unrestrained, eloquent, a rococo tirade against the object of
his anger (even a child, even a secretary) and everything it
represented, appalling, astonishing, frightening, delicious.
His fists clenched, but until the end he never hit me.

I can say, Well, he did it, not me. What I thought about
was that when they were with me, their lives were orderly
and low-key. I hardly ever got mad at them as I had when
we were all a family. Most of what they did was fine with
me. Away from Pat, I was without anger, without that
grating supervision, the constant call for my attention and
response. I was no longer the pivot between the boss and
the peons, responsible to everyone, the miraculous frag-
menting woman, pulled apart every day only to be knitted
together every night so that she could be pulled apart again
in the morning.

I never really probed into how he treated them, or even
imagined it, beyond remembering how he had been. That
was the realistic course of action, wasn't it?

But when I stepped out from between father and children,
not knowing, but not not knowing, either, I left them to
their own devices, didn't I? Whoever did it, they were damaged, weren't they? Here is something I remember about

Ed. A year went by, and I fell out of love with him, and another year went by, and another, and finally he moved away. In those three years I saw him from time to time, and every time I saw him I became nothing again. Even after I realized that he had intended none of this, that his cruelty was compounded of fear and shame, not disapproval and antagonism, his presence negated me. Damaged, he damaged me. A small thing. Smaller, by far, than the damage I did to Pat, than the damage we did to our children. "Is that a sigh?" says Joe from the front seat.

"The deepest," I say.

"Here we are," he says, turning in the driveway. "We survived, Mom," he says.

"What?" I say.

"What?"

"What did we survive?"

Michael opens his door and the overhead light goes on, revealing Joe turned in his seat, looking at me. He says, "Everything so far." His smile is lovely and rueful.

"Oh, I don't know," says Michael. He closes the door and the light goes off. I can see Joe's profile, his gaze intent upon his twin. All I can see of Michael is the back of his head framed in the windshield, his right hand stroking the wheel for a moment, then dropping.

"What?" says Joe, a single, tender syllable.

Michael clears his throat. "You knew I got engaged." Joe nods. "Then she broke it off." Joe nods again.

"I didn't know that," I exclaim.

Michael looks at me.

"I thought Joe would tell you, Mom. I kept meaning to write and tell you about Margaret, who is Scottish, very—" He glances around the car, hunting for the words, I think, then stares at me for a second before saying, "She's perky. No, she's dauntless, and sort of legendarily good. Anyway, there was another part. I don't think I mentioned, um, Lucie, even to Joe. She was the school director's wife. She's French, about thirty-five. They have four children." He turns and looks at me. "Nothing about this was pretty, Mom."

"Probably not."

"As soon as Margaret and I announced our engagement, Lucie began to flirt with me." He coughs. "She was seductive and experienced and all that, but the fact was that she was also quite fragile, and I knew it. She hated India, and I knew it. There was something about Margaret she didn't like. But, however much she wanted to try me out, or to put Margaret down, or to have fun, about a million times more than that, I wanted her. Every time I was with Margaret, and we had a happy, rollicking time, joking, talking, eating, laughing in bed, all these good things that I've been looking for for years, I couldn't wait to find Lucie. What I wanted to do with Lucie was to penetrate her beyond the possibility of penetration. I wanted to penetrate her organs and cells and atoms. She wanted that, too, after she saw what was possible. We had this pity for what we were doing to each other that was so piercing. We cried a lot. Margaret started crying, too, when she found out, but I always thought, She'll take care of herself. There was no way that Margaret, whom I loved, could pierce me, and no way that Lucie, whom I didn't love, could fail to pierce me. I asked Margaret to give me a month. I thought I could teach myself to flip the switch. On would be Margaret. Off would be Lucie. I would just drill myself into it. I would get things right, and then we would follow our plan to leave and travel and just be together. But Lucie turned out to be pregnant. She hadn't slept with her husband in a long time, so it looked like there would be quite a scandal. Margaret broke off with me."

"Well," says Joe.

"How long ago was this?" I say.

"Not very."

"What about the baby?"

"Lucie had an abortion. Margaret took her, since she was the only person who knew about the baby besides me."

"When was that?" says Joe.

"About ten days ago."

"Oh, boy," says Joe.

I realize as he speaks that I have sensed something beyond his fatigue and disorientation that obviously must be grief. But beyond that, like mountains beyond mountains, I recognize the settled darkness of expectation that grows from such desperate events. I recognize a possession of mine that I'd hoped my children would never claim.

In the kitchen Joe makes another pot of coffee. Michael pulls out one of those little cigars tied with red thread and begins to smoke it, standing next to the screen door, and letting the smoke waft out into the night. He leans against the jamb, his knee bent, his foot on the wall, like a man against a lamppost, and the beam of the single light above the sink drenches him with just that loneliness. Joe is taking cups out of the cabinet. Two. His hand pauses for an instant before reaching for the third one. I say, "I've been up since five myself. I guess I should go to bed." I am happy enough to vacate at this late hour, and there is undoubtedly some brotherly, twinly, comfort or companionship that only Joe can offer. Surely that is what an identical twin is for, after all. My own mood is suspended, floating.

I turn and go out of the room, but, I admit it, I pause in the dark hallway, where they can't see me, and watch them. Joe sets the cups down beside the coffeemaker and starts to pour the coffee. Michael pinches the end of the cigar, then tosses it out the door. Everything about his demeanor contrasts with Joe's. I can't believe I haven't recognized it before now. He did use to share Joe's nervousness, but now he is hard and knowing. Composed in spite of his utter weariness. His head swings round and he regards his brother.

He opens his mouth to speak, but just then Joe looks up and smiles, and he says nothing. What he wants to say is something that he can't say while Joe is looking at him. He licks his lips. Joe goes to the refrigerator for the milk. When he disappears behind the door, Michael says, "Before I left India, I signed a contract to go to Korea. Another two-year contract, teaching math." I step just the littlest bit farther out of their range—Michael's tone is as intimate as a lover's and as full of the knowledge that he is giving more pain than he is feeling. Joe closes the refrigerator and stands up without the milk. He looks at Michael. Michael continues, "The thing is, the school year starts in early September. The tenth."

It strikes me that my mother must have seen this composure in me, too, just before she died, when I knew where the children were but didn't know if I was ever going to see them again. I wonder if, as I am now, she was stricken, yet distantly relieved that her child had attained the end of inexperience.

"Is that the tenth our time?" says Joe.

"No, that's the ninth our time."

"Just tell me when you signed it."

"End of May."

"Our time?"

"Our time."

"You've written me five letters and never told me any of this."

"I guess, yeah."

"All that time I was writing about looking for an apartment for you and Margaret."

"Yeah."

"Before I sent you that course catalogue."

"I told you I wasn't that interested in graduate school. That's much more up your alley."

"Well, I guess I don't know what's up your alley anymore, do I?"

Michael inhales deeply and tips his head back against the wall.

Finally, Joe says, "Do you WANT to go?"

"Yeah."

Joe's voice rises a little. "Do you want to fall in love with some Korean woman, and have kids, and live there forever? That's what you're going to do, you know."

"Yeah."

"Yeah, what?"

"Yeah, I know. Yeah, I do. I do want to." They stare at each other. Michael says, "Hey, I'm going outside, all right? Just for some air. All right?"

"Who's stopping you?"

Michael pivots out the door and it slaps behind him. Joe pulls out a chair and sits at the table, staring fixedly at the door. Maybe it is the talk of Ed, the thoughts of Pat, many people leaving, many people left, but I know exactly what he is feeling, as if no time at all had passed, as if shock and pain could rush out of the memory as well as into it, scarify the nerves all over again. It is as if, in our family, the one necessary presence that each of us fixes on is the one presence each of us cannot have.

I back away, toward the stairway, as silently as possible. If Joe cries I don't want to know it.

Pat loved dinnertime. Although he didn't believe in God, he always said the Catholic grace, all the way down to "May the souls of the faithful departed through the mercy of God rest in peace." Then he took a deep breath, grinned, and surveyed the table—five stair-step heads, me wiping my hands on a dish towel as I sat down, the dogs, shiny black and alert, watching the spoon in his hand as he dished up the food. If there were relatives visiting, so much the better. If, temporarily, we had household help, they would be sitting at the table with us. If I was pregnant, he would call out to the unborn child, "Green beans tonight! You're going to like green beans someday! And here's corn on the cob!" He was such a young man, so handsome and smart. His enthusiasm for family life was the passion, I see now, of a true egomaniac, whose wife and children and dogs are the limbs of his own body. "Rachel?" he would say. "Rachel, are you listening? Ellen, tell her again." His eyes would probe mine until I couldn't return his gaze. Looking back, it is hard to sort out what I knew then from what I learned later. Certainly I had no intentions, only appetites.

He wanted a response, but I couldn't speak, knowing how acutely he would hear me, how clearly he would know from whatever I was saying what I was thinking. After a while, I couldn't even hear, although I tried to listen. I was a slow-burning fuse, but a fuse nonetheless, who could not fail to blow up the little gathering around the table. Aloft we went, spinning head over heels. There is no getting over it, for me or for them; there is only, I suppose, adding to it. With luck, balancing it. However my life looks to others, what it looks like to me is a child's tower of blocks, built in ignorance and without a plan.

I wonder if my father and uncles recognized their desires, or if they only recognized their duties: when desire expressed itself, in the form of my aunt, they contained it by force and made sure it never expressed itself again. Their lives always frightened me—wordless and monolithic, as if my uncles were not men but mere features of their own flat landscape. And so I guided myself by the light of my desires, as Pat, too, did, and from us our children have learned the same thing. Even so, we have not always known what we wanted, or not often known what we wanted, or not EVER known what we wanted, only that we wanted.

I think of Joe's smile as he told me that we had survived everything so far. I don't like to make too much of this. As Joe would say, children are starving and all that. He will survive this. Michael will survive this disaster as well as whatever drives him away and deadens him inside as he goes. Ellen will stay married or be drawn to divorce, the thing she loathes the most and can't get out of her mind. Whatever she does, she will survive it.

Even so, as I sit on my bed and pull off my stockings and rub my fifty-two-year-old toes, I think that I, too, have done the thing I least wanted to do, that I have given my children the two cruelest gifts I had to give, which are these, the experience of perfect family happiness, and the certain knowledge that it could not last.

GOOD WILL

1. ❦ *August*

During the first part of the interview, when we are sitting on the porch looking down the valley, I try for exactitude more than anything—$343.67. She is impressed, which pleases me, makes me impressed with myself, and then ashamed, so I say, "And seventy four cents of that I found, so I really made only $342.93. I suppose there might be a few more pennies somewhere, in a pocket or something." She writes it down with a kind of self-conscious flourish of her pen—a Bic "round stic," ten for ninety-nine cents, plus tax, if you buy them at the beginning of the school year— and I can see that momentary pause while she inventories all the things about her that she couldn't have if her income for last year were, like mine, $343.67. The view at the far end of the valley, the scattered houses of Moreton against the west face of Snowy Top, clears suddenly of August haze, and a minute later I feel a strong southwesterly breeze. Rain by mid-afternoon.

The other subjects in her book, some Seed-Save people, a tree-fruits fanatic, a raised-bed specialist, a guy who's breeding field corn back to its prehistoric varieties, all of them are going to be included for innovative gardening. Me I don't think she would have used if I'd had an outside job, or if Liz, my wife, had a job. We are no more up-to-date than Rodale, and she, that is, Tina, the interviewer, will know my methods from looking at the beds. But the money. That gets her. I say, "Before Tommy was born, our income usually hovered around a hundred and fifty dollars a year. But you simply can't raise a kid on a hundred and fifty dollars a year." A kid likes to have nice school supplies, for example. In September I expect to go to K-mart and spend six dollars or so on school supplies. Tommy likes the trip. He chooses very carefully.

The gardens lie around the house in a giant horseshoe, five ranges, forty-five separate beds of plants, some neat, some shaggy, all productive. There is nothing to brag about, to her; she knows her stuff, and anyway, this time of year everyone looks like a terrific gardener. The plants are thick and hung with fruit, but not unusual. She fingers the leaves, pulls some soil out from under the mulch, looks for pests. There are a few, but not many. I rely on companion plant-ing, crop rotation, garden sanitation. It works, but she doesn't ask about it. The praise she has to offer is in the sensuality and pleasure of her gestures, the way she lingers over each bed.

This is better. I didn't like the way the focus was so clearly on the money before. Money is the precise thing Liz and I don't focus on, which is why we earn so little. As soon as you bring up the money, I notice, conversation gets soci-ological, then political, then moral. I would rather talk about food, or swimming, or turkey hunting, or building furni-ture. The thing to do would be to get Liz to say, "Oh, Bob can make anything," in that factual way she has, explanatory rather than boastful, but Liz is offended by the whole in-terview process, by the light it shines on our lives and the way it makes a story of us. My promise to her was that Tina wouldn't ask her any questions and that she and Tommy wouldn't have to appear in any photographs.

The fact is, I should like this unaccustomed view of the Miller family, Robert, Elizabeth, and Thomas, on their small but remarkably productive acreage just outside Moreton, Pennsylvania. The fact is that years ago, when I had first bought the land and was building the big compost heaps behind the chicken shed, I used to imagine some interviewer just like Tina passing through, showing just her degree of dignity, respectability, and knowledgeable interest. I used to plan how I would guide her around the beds, then undug, show her through the house, then unbuilt, seat her in the chairs, feed her off the table, entertain her on the porch, and through imagining her, I saw all the details she might like. I imagined I would tell her, as I did during the interview, that imagination itself was the key—once I knew what it was specifically that I wanted, then either I would build it or it would turn up. And here she is, though I stopped looking for her long ago, right on schedule, reacting as she was destined to react. The pleasure of that is a private one, not one Liz would share, but not one I am inclined to give up, either.

It's true that I even foresaw that she would focus on the money. That's what I focused on myself then, how I had bought this great piece of land at an estate sale for only thirty-three hundred dollars, that was about sixty dollars an acre, as if all the acres were interchangeable. The bargain was precious, a good omen, a substitute for knowing what I was doing. Now the land has a personality, is without dollar value, and each acre is simply more or less useful or beautiful or ripe for improvement. The money embarrasses me. I should have been less exact. I should have said, "We made some. Enough. I don't know how much." But there is false humility in that, too, since I do know how much, since I do pay property taxes and buy school supplies and Tommy's yearly ticket on the school bus. Tina stands up and stares down the valley, then takes a deep breath. As we turn toward my workshop, she says, "This spot is paradise, isn't it?"

On my grandfather's farm in Ohio, the shop was neater than the kitchen, the tools shone more brightly than the silverware. For me, still, my workshop is apart from everything else. We try to cultivate orderly habits, but I don't mind the ebb and flow of schoolbooks, projects, articles of clothing, or toys through the house. Piles accumulate, are disposed of. Here nothing accumulates. When I am not working, the place looks like a museum exhibit—galleries of narrow shelves holding planes, chisels, knives, joiner's saws, files, hammers, mallets, rulers, gouging tools, sandpaper. Light pours through the open skylight and the window above the workbench. Each space is neatly labeled, identifying the resident tool, calling out for any absent one. The floor is swept (Liz made the broom one year, didn't like it in the house, and sent it out here). In a way this workshop is money, since it contains an irreplaceable treasury of tools, but other than the sandpaper, every item came to me as a gift, an inheritance, or a castoff. The planes, for example, with their thick beechwood stocks and blue steel blades, have been outmoded by table saws and routers, and auctioneers at farm sales used to thank me for taking them away by the basketful. I refinished the stocks and reseated the hardware. Now I am told people ransack antique stores for old planes to give their living rooms that "country" look. I could not afford to replace these. Tina glances around politely, and says, "Lovely," before stepping back outside and staring at the gardens again. When I join her, she remarks, "The best carrot germination I ever got was fifty percent, and that was the time I nicked each seed with a file." I cough. Carrot seed is about the size of beach sand.

Liz waves to me from the porch. Lunch is ready. Although she disapproves of the interview, she wants to please the visitor. She has asked me every day about the menu for lunch, about whether she should bake the sourdough bread from whole wheat or white flour (our biggest expense after property taxes), whether I think any melons will be ready, what the chances are that Tina will be repelled by the wild foods—purslane, blackberries, angelica—that we eat routinely and enjoy. I, on the other hand, have been wanting to impress. "I built that chest from a black walnut Liz and I chopped down ourselves. I found the axle and the wheels for that wagon in the junkyard. I built the box myself. We caught these trout this morning. We gave up row planting before any books came out about it." My own bragging voice followed me around to every job for days. It cannot be done, this task I give myself, the task of communicating the pleasures of our life in this valley, even to an ear that longs to hear of them.

I would begin with the weight and cottony fragrance of the quilts we've made, an "All Hands Around" on the bed, a big log cabin in rainbow colors against black on the wall. In sixteen years we've made twelve quilts, used up one, burned a hole in another. In the winter we use two or three for warmth, and the first thing I see in the morning, in the white light of our whitewashed bedroom, is the clashing colors of the quilts spilling away from me over the bed. Then, under my feet, I feel the smooth-painted floorboards. The windows are uncurtained and unshaded, usually flat gray with morning fog. All of this is familiar and comforting.

Or I could begin with something even more inexpressible, which would be the stiffness of muscles worked the day before and sensed afresh a moment after waking. I think my consciousness must rouse before my senses, because there is always, always, a pain-free moment, and then the ache flows in. I like the ache. It tells me what I did yesterday, suggests what I might do today, even how I might do it. Farm work doesn't have to be backbreaking. It can be as aerobically sound and healthfully taxing as any other sort of exercise. Liz calls this "spading-as-sport" my private obsession, but another early morning pleasure is her sleepy, admiring rake of fingertips over my pectorals and abdominals.

Or there's Tommy's room, when I pass his doorway first thing in the morning, when Tommy is thoroughly asleep. He seems afloat in his bed, under his quilt, a green, orange, and yellow "Rail Fence." On the shelves I built are the toys we made him. He sleeps in a shirt Liz wove (I built the loom) on a straw tick the three of us stuffed. Across the room he has known since birth is the rocking cradle I copied, in local butternut, from a picture in a book I got out of the library. The headboard and footboard trim is carved with a twist, to look like a piece of rope; then the twist is repeated in the four braces that hold up the cradle. The lambskin lying across the mattress Liz made came from one of our lambs. The lamb's wool of the baby blankets was spun from some of the others. Liz's mother taught me to crochet, and I used to crochet while Liz knitted. When I look into my son's room, my pleasure is the knowledge that I have brought all of my being to bear here—not just hands and brain, but seed, too, and not just seed, but hands and brain, too. If he were really afloat, his bed would bump against the window, and he could look upon the orchard I planted, then bump against the shelves I built, where he could snatch down tops and cars and blocks and tools and dolls we've made him; this is a lovely sea, I think, tiny, enclosed, friendly, all his, and his alone.

Lunch doesn't look too weird—a plate of sliced tomatoes and green peppers, a couple of trout, cold boiled potatoes, beet greens, blackberries. Tommy follows his mother back and forth between the range and the table in a way I find annoying, and so I say, "Son, sit down!" He tenses, smiles,

sits down. He is a good boy. Tina sits beside him and he offers her the pitcher of cold springwater, as he should. She looks around the room.

I can't help it. I lean back in my chair and say, "You know, it's remarkable what I've gleaned for free over the years. We have fishing rods and ponies and bicycles, a canoe, plenty of tools, sheep, two goats, lots of chickens. We tried a couple of turkeys a few years ago, and a cow, but she gave too much milk. This house has double-hung windows, figured brass doorknobs, a front door with a big pearly oval of etched glass. An old man in State College gave me that kitchen range. It's from the twenties. He found it in his barn. A guy I know in Moreton hauled it for me, in exchange for three lambs. It cooks our food and keeps the entire house warm. The first five years I lived here I spent getting to know people and offering things, then asking for things they were about to discard. Now, when people for miles around want to get rid of something, they send me a card. Incoming mail is free. Every so often I jerk loose and buy a couple of dollars' worth of stamped postcards for replies." I smile. "Compared to scrounging in Vietnam, which I did, this is no big deal."

We begin helping ourselves to the food. Tina asks, "What do you do for transportation?" Her manner is mild. I was the one looking forward to this, so I'm not sure why it puts me on edge. I say, "We think about it."

Liz doesn't like my brusqueness. She smiles and says, "He means that we plan ahead. Most days nobody goes anywhere except Tommy to school on the school bus, anyway."

"If I have a job or am trading something, part of the bargain is that they come here and pick me or it up. Besides, it's only three miles to town. We can walk or ski. Tommy can ride the pony." The tomatoes are delicious, sweet and firm and juicy. I never plant hybrids, only old fashioned

varieties like Rutgers and Marglobe and Roma. I save the seed from the best plants and best fruits, selecting for hardiness and flavor. It works. "The thing is, going away should be something you contemplate, not something you do automatically."

"Could you live this way farther back in the mountains?"

"You mean, where it's colder, harder to get places, and rockier?"

"Yeah."

"You really mean, if not this extreme, then why not more extreme, as extreme as possible? Why not Alaska or the Australian outback?"

"I didn't mean that, but why not?"

"Why not really live off the land. Grubs and ants and spearing fish with a sharpened stick."

"Bob, come on," Liz says; then she turns to Tina. "We went through that about five years ago. Bob kept looking at brochures about land in Montana and British Columbia."

"We didn't ever send in the business reply cards, though. I was joking then, I'm joking now. My purposes aren't extreme, or political. My aim wasn't to choose the hardest path and prove I could do it. It was the same as everyone else's aim. It was to prosper. You don't prosper on hilly, rocky soil. It's more expensive to live in town or far from town, less expensive to live outside of town. We're self-contained, not isolated and hostile."

Tommy relishes everything on his plate, not preferring the sweet to the savory, the cooked to the fresh, the domestic to the wild. He is a model eater, would devour grubs and ants and roots if they were on the table. Can Tina see what a miraculous child he is, how enthusiastic and open and receptive to guidance? Before he was born, I used to imagine a child-raising program that was purely example-setting. I would go about my work and he would accompany me, gradually assuming responsibility for the tasks that he was

strong enough and smart enough for. There would be a lot of informative conversation, I thought—me explicating techniques and him asking intelligent questions. The reality is better than that. He tags along as eagerly as anyone could hope for, but he does all the talking. A lot of it is questions, but much of it is observations, remarks, little stories, bits of songs that are going through his head. There is a large category of stray sounds that simply escape his lips, from grunts to hisses to yells that I hope he has the sense to contain when he is at school but that I like for their animal quality, for their way of saying, "This organism is alive."

Which is not to say that example-setting is sufficient. I find that he does need a lot of molding and guidance, but that is another task we plan for, Liz and I.

After lunch there is a routine of work—bringing the animals into the barn out of the sun, checking water buckets, looking for eggs—that I think Tina should accompany me on, but when we sit back in our seats, Liz speaks up and says, "Tina and I will clear this up. Why don't you and Tommy come back in an hour for a swim?"

Considering that, when I asked her what she thought about this interview a couple of weeks ago, she said that she would rather chase pigs in a snowstorm, I am a little surprised. But it is a relief. Tommy runs out ahead of me, knowing that after chores he can ride the pony for half an hour before his rest time. He doesn't notice the view, but I do; every time the screen door slaps shut behind me, I pause and stare down the valley meadow toward Moreton, Snowy Top, and the dusky receding folds of the mountains beyond. My land is laid out rather deceptively—the smallest part is open field, valley floor, but all of these acres are visible from the house, and all of them are flat. The slope from the foot of the valley to the house is only three degrees, which is unusual around these parts. There has always been a farm on this site, and the barn remains, though the original

house burned down in 1904—it was a big house and a big fire that the volunteer fire department could see from town but couldn't get to, because over a mile of the road was drifted in. One of the children ran burning from the house, but they rolled him in the snow and saved his life. The article took up half the front page of the Moreton *Record.* The family moved in with relatives in town, and their descendants farmed from there—keeping this land in pasture for seventy years, and running sheep and heifers and horses on it. When I bought it, the soil was so well fertilized that all I had to do the first year was turn under the turf and dig the beds. The other outbuildings were pretty up-to-date, too: the lean-to workshop beside the barn, a well-ventilated root cellar ten feet from the foundation of the old house (when I scraped dirt and caked mud off the old door, I found its surface scorched black from the fire, but the shelves inside that once held bins of vegetables were only dusty).

Most of the land I own runs up the hillsides in a bowl shape, to either side and behind the house, and that woodlot hadn't been touched or exploited in seventy, or even a hundred years. It took me three years just to drag the deadfall out, and I heated my house for seven and a half years on that. If I'd had the stone masonry built around the range that I have now, it would have lasted twice that long. What we do is build our first fire in mid-September, then make sure a small fire is in the stove every minute thereafter. All that masonry will have heated up by about mid-October, and after that we only have to keep it warm. It works. I use a lot less wood than the woodlot produces, and it's all hardwood. We even burn black walnut and cherry, wood the cabinetmaking companies would pay me for if they knew I had it. That's my luxury, my conspicuous consumption—I burn black walnut for heat.

From the house, everything is perfect. The natural landscape offers enclosed, familiar, pleasing curves, softened

with August haze and prolific vegetation—sugar maple, black cherry, hickory, butternut, walnut, beech, yellow birch, and white oak are some of what I can see from here—and I respond, unfailingly, with love ("regard" and "inspiration," looking and inhaling). From everywhere else on the property, I must view my own mistake, the house. I built it—yes, I built it—mostly from brick torn out of the streets of State College, Pennsylvania, and pine pallets that I ripped the nails out of one by one. Recognizing my accomplishment doesn't mean I've ever been satisfied with it. I resent its lack of grandeur more than its lack of size. What I meant to keep simple I made humble, and I made a mistake siting it, because I thought it would be easier to use the old foundation than lay another one. If we were to add on now, we would have to add outward, creating an ungainly, flat building. If I'd built farther back—into the hillside as I first intended—it would have been easy to add on upward, just to tear off the roof and build another small house on top of the old one. And we would have been closer to the spring-house. Sometimes I can see the structure I might have built so clearly that the frustration of what I've done is explosive. Here we live, here we will always live. No gardens, barns, sheds will ever mitigate the permanence of this mistake.

Chores completed, I return. The women are sitting at the table, still, talking about home schooling. Tina looks skeptical, which makes Liz speak more assertively, expressing none of the doubts she has expressed to me. Home schooling is my idea, and her arguments are ones I've made to her. "Actually," she is saying, "studies show that they get along better with the other kids once they get to college, because they have a real sense of themselves and a sense of their own abilities."

"But don't they miss the other kids?"

"I don't know if Tom would. We sent him to kindergarten, because we felt guilty about keeping him so isolated.

He gets along okay, but until you've really considered home schooling, I don't think you realize what a compromise school is, how regimented it is, and how the others expect you to act so you'll fit in. And around here there's nothing to do, so most of the high-school kids gather at one of the big ponds and drink, then drive around endangering themselves and everyone else. It's not like a big suburban school, where they might be, only might be, exposed to something new."

"Well, social life has meant a lot to Libby since she's been in kindergarten—"

Libby must be a daughter. They have covered a lot of ground in my absence, and I am sort of shocked by the name, "Libby," rather idle-rich-sounding, as if this project of Tina's is a whimsy after all, not committed or serious as it would be if she had no children, or her daughter's name was, say, Susie.

"But she's a girl. Bob was a loner in school. I wasn't. I think I missed more than he did. I just had the same experiences everyone else had. I don't feel like my life had any integrity until I came here."

"It's lovely—"

"And you know, at first I hated it. I didn't have any inner resources at all. I thought I would die of loneliness, even on days when Bob would talk to me." She smiles slyly at me. "This was not how I intended to spend my life."

"I just think it takes a lot of fortitude to have your child at home, to be responsible for everything that goes into his head. What does Tommy think?"

Now I speak up. "He likes the idea, but we promised him one more year in the grammar school before we make up our minds."

Liz glances at me. I make the truthful emendation. "Well, he doesn't always like it. But his schooling is my decision to make. He understands that. Anyway, we're a closely knit

family, and there's so much going on around here all the time that he doesn't want to miss anything. And as for taking responsibility for what goes into his head, that AT-TRACTS me."

Tina sits back. She says, "Your lives are so completely of a piece. I admire—"

"You know, I always think I'm going to love being ad-mired, but then I get nervous when it happens, I think because you shouldn't be admired for doing something you needed to do. I mean, until I moved here, I was so filled with frustrated yearning that it was this or suicide. When I was Tommy's age, I thought it was yearning to be on my own. When I was a teenager, I thought it was lust. When I was in the army, and in Vietnam, I thought it was the desire to go home. But it was none of those things. I never figured out what it was, but it ceased. Tommy doesn't have it. He's enthusiastic about the farm and the animals and fishing and helping us cook and grow things, everything we do here that we couldn't do if we lived in town." Just now the rain begins, steady and warm, lifting the scent of the grass, of the valley's whole morning, through the screen door—wildflowers, tomato plants, walnut leaves, pony and sheep manure, the rainwater itself. It is a smell so thick and various that I can nearly see it, and I inhale sharply. Liz laughs and leans toward Tina. "Put this in your book. Bob pretends to have opinions, but the real truth about him is that his senses are about three times sharper than normal. He's really just a farm animal scratching his back in the dust."

"Not true!" I say. "What I really am is a body attached to a pair of hands that can't stop making things. Inclination precedes conviction. I want to make, therefore I decided making is valuable. The more I want to make, the more valuable making is."

"Very nice, sweetie," says Liz, standing up and kissing

the top of my head. "But running your hand down the board precedes making."

Tommy appears on the porch, dripping, but doesn't come in. He calls, "Hey, Daddy, I got the pony and the foal in before the rain started! They didn't get wet at all!"

"Did you wipe off the bridle?"

"Yes, Daddy."

"Even the corners of the bit?"

"Yes, Daddy."

Liz hands him a towel and he dries off in the doorway. He has what we call "the look." His face is too bright, his eyes too eager; a kind of rigidity seems to grip him when he is still, but when he moves, the movements are quick and broad. Liz recognizes it, too, and says, patiently, "Sweetie, time to settle down for your rest. You want some milk before you go up? Sit by Daddy, and I'll pour you some."

He might sit. He might run into the other room. He might knock over his chair. I must have had the look, too, when I was his age, because I remember the feeling perfectly, a feeling of imminent eruption, fearsome, alluring, uncontrollable. It was like standing in a dim, warm, small room and having an astonishing bright light switched on every so often, and when the light was on I couldn't remember what it was like for the light to be off. From the ages of about nine to about twelve, I worked steadily to lighten the room molecule by molecule, until the bright light no longer shocked me, and the room glowed comfortably. What I actually did I can't remember, but I remember the sensation of light, the feeling of having labored, and my father remarking that I had gotten to be a good boy after all, no longer "all over the place like a crazy person." My first real feeling of accomplishment, the first time I knew that I could master myself.

Perhaps because of Tina, Tommy sits quietly, drinks his

milk, and doesn't knock over his chair until he stands up. Liz picks it up with ostentatious care and I say, "Time for your rest, son. When you come down, I want you to show me the chapter you've read."

"How many pages?"

"A whole chapter."

"Even if it's ten pages?"

"A whole chapter."

He contains himself and marches off. All of these things happen every day, and yet they seem so peculiar with Tina at the table, making notes in her head. I am tempted to apologize, but I don't know for what, so I hold my tongue.

When we are undressing that night for bed, I admit it, that the interview was a bad idea. "I mean, I hate feeling this detached from everything. Look at my foot going under the covers. Look at my hands pulling the blankets up, aren't these lovely quilts, look at my wife, 'Liz' she's called, blowing out the lamp."

Liz laughs, reaches under the covers to tickle me lightly. "She thought you were a genius."

"What?"

"You heard me."

"When did she say that?"

"After lunch, then again before she left. She said, 'Everything he touches he transforms into something beautiful and useful.' "

"What did you say?"

"I said that I agreed."

"You did?"

She runs her hand over my face in the darkness, a gesture that is tender and proprietary at the same time. She says, "I told her I hoped she put that in the book, because that's what's true about you."

After we make love, when I am nearly asleep, I feel her ease out of bed, then I feel her turn, kneel beside the bed,

and begin to pray. I hear that murmuring all night, even after I know in my sleep that her solid weight is unconscious beside me.

The next day is Saturday. At breakfast, Liz says, "You remember about the church meeting this afternoon?"

"I remember."

"I'll be home about six, unless someone gives me a ride to the end of the road. I might be home by five-twenty or so."

"Fine."

"Really?"

"Liz, you don't have to ask. It's fine."

"Good. I'm looking forward to it."

About a year ago, Liz started shopping around for a church to attend. There are ten churches in Moreton and she went to every one, judging them more on ambience than on doctrine. The two Quaker congregations, having within living memory been one, were hyper-aware of each other, she said, the Episcopalians enjoyed themselves too much, the Presbyterians were engaged in easing out their minister, and on down the line, until she decided upon the "Bright Light Fellowship," a Pentecostal sect whose prophet resides in Gambier, Ohio. I was frankly astonished that my wife, a graduate of the University of Pennsylvania and a voracious reader, could feel at ease in this collection of the rural poor, the badly educated, and the nakedly enthusiastic, but that is exactly what she feels there, she says. Privately, I think she feels humbled, which is a feeling she is in favor of as a way of life. She began participating in January, and attended every Sunday. If it snowed, she went on skis; if it rained, she wore rubber boots and a poncho. She asks me if I mind. I do, but I would rather not, and I certainly don't want to influence her. Nevertheless, it has become one of those marital topics of conversation, a rift that we consciously avoid making an argument of. My own

religious views are deistic, you might say. I notice that days when she goes to church, for whatever reason, are special days, obstructing the smooth flow of time that I like. She assumes that this is my main objection. I also notice that, however else she arranges and varies her time with, and communication with, Tommy and me, she never fails to kneel at bedtime and make a lengthy prayer. That, both the unfailing regularity of it, and the awkwardness of its insertion into our nightly routine, is the real bone of contention. I have been married to Liz for a long time—twelve years —and I intend to be married to her forever, so I am cautious about drawing any conclusion as to whether this issue is a passing one, one that can be resolved through compromise, or simply a large, heavy object that sits in the living room, obstructing traffic, grudgingly accommodated, year after year.

Of course I have forgotten about the church meeting, so my response, because there has to be one, is to hold a little aloof—to go out in the workshop and dive into a project of my own rather than to do something more friendly, like sort iris corms on the front porch. What I do is remind myself that I am a genius, and, when I step into the workshop, that lends even these kitchen chairs I am making the glow of loveliness. They are made from ash saplings, with woven rush seats, and my tools are, basically, my draw knife and a bucket of water. There are chairs like them in every antique store—rounded stiles, ladder-backs, four stretchers below the seat—but mine are the only comfortable ones I've ever sat in. The seat is roomier, for one thing, and I soak the stiles and angle them backward so that you don't feel like you're about to be strapped in and electrocuted. I soak all the mortise joints, too, before I put everything together, and they dry and shrink around the tenon so tightly that the whole chair might have been carved from a single piece of wood. These are almost finished. All I have left is a carving of leaves and vines into the top rung of the ladder-back.

Well, it is a pleasant day. I sit on one of the chairs I've made and decorate another one. The chestnut tree above me is alive with light and shade, the weather is warm and breezy, my wife and son go about their business with evident satisfaction. The valley that is our home is soothingly beautiful, safe, and self-contained. We eat a lunch that we have provided for ourselves, and afterward I am so involved with my carving that I forget Liz is gone until I see her come walking down the road, and then, no matter who she's been with, all I want to do is to meet her, kiss her, and walk her to the house.

"Guess what?" she says.

"I'm a genius?"

"Yeah. You know how I can tell?"

"How?"

"You forgot that school starts Tuesday."

"This Tuesday? I thought that wasn't till after Labor Day this year."

"Monday is Labor Day. It's been September for four days now."

"Tina was supposed to come on the fifteenth of August."

"Well, she was two weeks late and we didn't even notice. She ought to put that in her book."

"You went to church last Sunday. Didn't you realize what day it was?"

"It didn't come up. It's not like when you're a Catholic and you're always counting backwards or forwards to some major holiday."

"Well, I guess that shows that the prophet is a man of his time. He figures everybody knows what day it is."

"If you really want to know, what he figures is that every day might as well be the last."

We haven't talked about specifics of dogma very much,

but I let it drop. Anyway, Tommy comes out of the barn, where he has been haying and watering the ponies for the night, and greets his mother as if she has been gone since Christmas. She swings him up into her arms, and continues walking, his arms around her neck and his legs around her waist. The voice of my father tells me that he is too old for this, but my own voice disagrees, says that boys are isolated too soon, that as long as he seeks our bodies he should find them. And there is also this reassuring shiver of jealousy, a light touch raising the hairs on the nape of my neck, that reminds me how the pleasure of marriage and the pleasure of fatherhood take their piquancy from watching, left out, as they nuzzle and giggle and tease. He never tries to impress her; she never tries to mollify him. We haven't used birth control since our marriage and she only got pregnant once. Most of the time I forget that it could happen again. Secretly, I have only ever managed to imagine one boy child. Maybe imagination is the key there, too. "Lovely sunset," says Liz, and Tommy says, "We fried green tomatoes with basil for dinner."

"Mmm," says his mommy. "I just love that."

We stroll up the road toward the house, toward the dinner laid on the table, and this is what we expect: to eat and be satisfied, to find comfort in each other's company, to relinquish the day and receive the night, to make an orderly retreat from each boundary that contains us—the valley, the house yard, the house, the room, the covers, wakefulness —in perfect serenity. Well, of course I am thankful, and of course a prayer lifts off me, but there is nothing human about it, no generalizations, nor even words, only the rightness of every thing that is present expressing itself through my appreciation.

2. 🍂 *October*

I admit I like to be prepared for things. A life without money is predicated on anticipation (although, maybe, it is shaped by the unexpected). More that is unexpected happens when you are married, more still when you have a child. Mostly these unexpected things leave me confused and slow, which is what happens when the day rolls around for slaughtering the summer's lambs. I feel less than no compunction about slaughtering the lambs, because in fact they are no longer cunning little lambs, they are now stupid, homely sheep. A sheepskin, a leg of mutton, these are things of beauty to me. A flock of sheep trampling each other in a panic is not. They often panic. They often trample. My ram and my six ewes, which I got from a number of different sources, are unrelated to one another and produce healthy, mixed-breed lambs. Inbred animals are subject to parasites, disease, and immune system problems that I might not be able to control with garlic wormers, nutritious feed, and sanitary pasturing practices, so my lambs have no future in my flock.

I get up feeling good on the day I am to slaughter the sheep. Liz is perky, too, because there will be a lot of work to do. We throw some logs into the range, savor the morning chill. I am standing on a chair, rummaging through upper cupboards for my .45, a World War II service revolver

I found at an auction, and for the box of shells I bought last fall, when Tommy comes weeping into the kitchen.

Tommy is nearly eight; he has been present for eight sheep massacres, and cognizant for at least four, so it takes a while for me to understand that it is the death of the lambs that has upset him. When I do understand, I admit, I slam my fist down on the table, angered rather than gladdened that he has grown up enough in the past year to imagine the sheep's point of view. He sniffles over his breakfast. I shout, "Well, you are going to help! That's the lesson here. If you eat something, you have to help produce it. Do you want to be a vegetarian?"

He shakes his head. "Do you like lamb stew? Or trout? Or sausage?"

"Yes, Daddy."

"Well?"

"I don't want to."

"Want to what?"

"Watch you kill them."

"Why not?"

"I don't want to."

"Mr. John Doe, a guy who buys a steak at a grocery store. Don't know where it came from, don't know what it means to eat it. You want to be like that?"

"No, Daddy."

"We took good care of those lambs. They ate good grass and had plenty of fresh water, and now they won't know what hit them. This is a good life for a lamb, Tommy, all the way to the end and past it."

"I don't want to."

I stand up from the table. "Come on outside."

We shear the lambs first, getting a few pounds of lovely soft wool, and then I shoot them in the head and cut their throats to drain out the blood. We do a good job—quick, competent, without arousing much fear in the lambs. I even

take each one around the corner of the barn, out of sight of the others, to do the deed. By mid-afternoon eight lamb-skins are pegged to the back of the barn, and the cuts of meat are ready for my friend, Martin Summerbee, who picks it up, wraps it, and freezes it over the winter for me in exchange for half of it. Tommy has been so obedient—holding the lambs during the shearing, helping me hoist them by the feet and catch the blood after they are slaughtered—that I have forgotten, or dismissed, the morning's disagreement. That is a Saturday. On Wednesday he arrives home from school with a note from Miss Bussman, the second grade teacher. It reads,

Dear Mr. Miller,

This noontime, while the other children were at lunch, Tom went into the cloakroom and found some toys, two dolls that are owned by another child, Annabel Harris. He twisted these dolls until they broke apart, and tore some of their dollclothes. Annabel is aware that she should not have had the dolls in school, but Tom did take them out of her schoolbag. He says that he is sorry for what he calls "the accident." I have told Mrs. Harris that the dolls will be replaced. One is a "Jem" doll and one is a "Kimber" doll. I would like to speak with you about the incident. It has been most disturbing.

Sincerely,
Leona Bussman

Liz, reading over my shoulder, is the first to finish. She makes a little sound, between a cry and a groan, very soft, as she reads, but says nothing afterward, only turns back to the sink, where we have been washing clothes. Tom sits at the table, absolutely still, not even kicking his leg or

tapping his finger. I read the letter again, and say, "Were you that upset over the lambs, son?"

"What?" His surprise at this connection is genuine and total. If he doesn't make it, should I?

"I thought maybe you were still upset about the lambs, and so you thought this would be a good thing to do, to get back at me, or maybe just to express your anger."

"I don't care about the lambs. We kill the lambs every year."

"Then why would you do such a thing to somebody's toys? I'm surprised at you. It sounds from the note like you planned it for when the others were away."

"I knew she had those dolls."

"But why did you do it, Tommy?" Liz speaks softly from the sink. He gives her a long, careful look, then returns to looking at his foot. We wait. The kettle on the woodstove whistles, and Liz snatches it off the heat as if shushing it. We wait until he says, "She's a nigger."

Liz has a tone of voice that reminds me that her family once had money, a tone that suggests that it is unbearable to hear some things, and so they have not been heard. She uses it now. She says, "Pardon me?" There is no maternity in it, and it is meant to force the shame of repeating the unspeakable upon the perpetrator.

"She's a nigger." This time he speaks casually, and the toe-tapping, wiggling, sniffling, and fidgeting of little boyhood suddenly resume, like music after a long rest. My reach is enormous. My hands seem to myself to arc across the room and grab his shoulders like a bundle of sticks. His head snaps backward as I pull him to me, and then I do something I promised him two years ago that I would never again do, which is to lay him over my knees and whale the tar out of him. The words pop out in time to the blows: "NEVER. USE. THAT. WORD. IN. FRONT. OF. ME. AGAIN." At the end of one sentence, he slides off my lap, reduced from a little boy to nothing, weeping, clutching his bottom, gasping for air. But that image isn't as vivid as the other, his nonchalant defiance, and so it is all I can do to prevent myself from kicking him where he sobs under the table. Liz steps over to him in a businesslike fashion, takes his hand, and pulls him up. "Go to your room now," she says, "and we'll talk about it later."

It has been maybe ten minutes since he handed us the note. All the issues—the sheep, the dolls, the racial slur, his careless attitude, my violent reaction—seem to lie on top of one another, each discrete, none resolved, and each leading to the others in a way that prevents resolution, or even discussion. It would be wrong to provide him with an excuse for either the damage he has done or the language he has used, but his transgressions do seem to lie between my insistence that he help with the sheep and this spanking, expressing something about the triumph of my will on both these occasions. I was unprepared. The result is awkward confusion.

Liz says, from the sink, "I hated hearing him say that, but I don't know if it warranted violence."

"Maybe he'll never forget, at any rate."

"But we don't even know if he understands why you attacked him. You were so quick!"

"Everything about it was quick. Simultaneously, I was hearing that word, I was seeing the way he sat there, I was hearing him say that word in front of strangers and feeling their disapproval of us and this setup we have, I was imagining that little girl finding her broken dolls, I was imagining her showing them to her parents and what they would think of us, I was remembering being in the army, I was remembering that Faulkner story where they lynch the guy and seeing my own son in those characters." She smiles and comes over to me, puts her hand in my hair. This enables me to say, "I blew it, didn't I?"

"I don't know, Robert. I don't know what the right reaction is. Maybe the right reaction is the most natural one."

"I'm not inclined to think so."

Liz drops into a chair by the table. The fact is, this has exhausted us, but we still have to finish the washing, string lines over the range and hang the clothes, clean up after the washing, feed and water the animals, milk the goats, make dinner, clean up from dinner, make sure that Tommy does his homework, bring in wood, stoke the fire so it will last until morning, heat water for washing, warm our beds with bricks so that we can stand to get into them, and check the animals one last time for the night. I say, "Let's phone out for a pizza."

Liz says, "Let's phone out for a phone."

"Let's phone out for a road they can deliver it on."

"Let's phone out for a town with a pizza parlor in it."

"No," I say, "I guess I'd really rather have Chinese." Our laugh supplies just enough energy for us to hoist ourselves out of our chairs and get to work.

Later, when we have sorted through all the apologies and explanations and come to the real question, where did Tommy learn to call Annabel Harris a "nigger," he says, "That's what some teachers were calling her. I heard them. Miss Bussman, too."

"When did you hear it?"

"One day when we had personal reading and I was going to the boys' room. They were standing in the hall."

"When was it?"

"Pretty long ago. Some fifth-graders said it, too. They were standing in the boys' bathroom, and they said, 'Did you see that nigger girl in the second grade?' " He glances at me and licks his lips. "That was the first day of school."

"Do you remember what the teachers said exactly?"

"They were talking in soft voices."

There is something like ten dollars around the house, since I just paid my property taxes two weeks ago. Ten dollars may or may not buy replacement dolls. At any rate, there will be a lot of walking—to the school, to a phone so that I can call the Harrises, to some shopping center (the nearest is in State College)—and every trip will reveal to interested parties the defects of our way of life when it comes to coping with the unexpected.

The next day I get to the school just as the bus of home-bound children is pulling away. I haven't called ahead, and I want to be sure Miss Bussman is there. I find her straightening up the classroom. She is humming, but her manner hardens when she turns and sees me. She says, "Visitors should check in with the office."

"I'm Bob Miller, Tommy's father."

Now she relaxes, but her inspection of me is frank, as if suppositions are being confirmed. It is Liz who should have come. I say, "I guess we haven't met before. I don't have a car, so we don't very often get to the evening conference sessions. You know, where everybody gets to meet?"

She sits far away from me, doesn't smile or shake my hand. She is young, maybe twenty-five or -six. Last year Tommy's teacher was about my age. She at least remembered a time when others had the ambitions I had, but this one doesn't. She says, "Well, these actions of Tommy's have upset the whole class. And they've upset me, as well."

"Mrs. Miller and I were very surprised."

"Well, to be candid, Mr. Miller, I wasn't, really. Toward the beginning of the year, another thing happened, but I thought it had passed, and was forgotten. I was wrong, and I should have sent a note home to you then."

"What was that?"

"Well, one day, apropos of nothing, Tommy just spoke

up in class and said, 'How'd this nigger girl get in here?' I was shocked. And, actually, Annabel didn't really react. I'm not sure she's ever heard the word before, and I don't know that she realized he was talking about her."

"I wish you had let me know."

She smiles a tight, uncomfortable smile. "Well, Mr. Miller, I actually wasn't certain that you would care, I mean, that that sort of language would be unacceptable to you." She gives me a challenging glance.

"Miss Bussman, I can say with certainty that Tommy has never heard that word at home. In fact, he says he heard some of the teachers using that word early in the school year."

Miss Bussman's wide blond face closes over, and she says, "That's absurd, Mr. Miller." I should have begun with the fifth-graders in the bathroom. We stare at each other for a second, then look down at the table. The knowledge that someone is lying has already soured this discussion.

I gather my patience. The visceral knowledge that Tommy's teacher is predisposed against him, for whatever reason, makes me a little breathless. I say, heavily, "Well, thank you for talking to me. You shouldn't have any more trouble with him, and I'll arrange things with the Harrises about the dolls."

"Mrs. Harris. Just Mrs. Harris."

"Fine. I'll get her address."

"I have it." She holds me at the door, rummages through her purse for an endless time. The walls of the schoolroom are awash in construction paper and bright sayings: "The only bad question is a question never asked," "Have you smiled today?", "Reading Is Fun!" She says, "Route Three. The number is 453-9876." She holds my gaze, but there are no more even tight smiles; something has released the rein she was holding on her disapproval. Outside the school, my anger suddenly fires, not at Miss Bussman, but at Liz, for opposing home schooling and holding out for one more year.

I dredge a quarter out of my pants and call the number. "Dr. Harris," she keeps saying. "Dr. Harris." I am not even sure she hears what I have to say, although she does tell me where her place is, about a mile out, southwest of town. From there to my place it is about five miles over roads, three over the hills. By the clock in the drugstore it is already four. It will be dark by six. One thing Liz and I have trained ourselves to do is wait patiently. The other one WILL get home. But I am not looking forward to the long, dark walk I will have to make on an empty stomach, turning over the mystery of my son's misdeeds all the way.

The house is a nice one, built in the twenties, it looks like, with mullioned windows in the front and a little stream, Laurel Creek, running along the western edge of the property. Dr. Harris, or someone, has planted a lot of flower beds, and though they are frosted this late in the year, they tempt me to veer from my straight, narrow, and chastened path to the front door. The front entrance is one I could envy—two sidelights and a fanlight above. When I ring the bell, the hall chandelier blazes up, and its glitter pours through the fanlight onto the front porch. The door opens. A pleasant voice says, "Mr. Miller? Come on in."

Immediately it is apparent that Dr. Harris has the touch. The front hall and the living room leading off it are bright, warm, comfortable, and stylish. The high ceilings, painted pale, peachy rose, the white woodwork, the pale green walls, the graceful dark shine of the banister curling toward the second floor, the lamps, lit. I have lived without electricity for so long that the silvery gold light of the lamps enchants me. The furnishings aren't expensive, I would bet—the same mix of almost antiques and affordable new pieces that others I know around here have—but hers have been refinished and reupholstered to look bright and fresh.

Plants and dried-flower arrangements are grouped about. In a southern bay window I hadn't noticed from outside sit three gardenias. Two of them are blooming. I realize I am gawking. I look at Dr. Harris, who is dressed in peacock-blue sweatclothes. She is not pretty, but her face has a pleasant, knowing look. Her hair is pulled back, giving her head a sculptured quality. I wonder what she knows. I would give anything to find out that she thinks the incident of the dolls is just little boy mischief that could have happened to any girl, nothing directed at Annabel herself, nothing perpetrated by Tommy himself.

I say, "I came to apologize for Thomas. If it weren't such a long walk, I would have brought my son, but we don't own a car."

"Thank you, Mr. Miller. If the dolls hadn't been new for Annie's birthday, she wouldn't have had them at the school—" She pauses. "They're silly dolls. Have you seen them? Members of a girls' rock band. Worse than Barbie." She smiles. "Maybe your son was esthetically offended."

"Thanks, but you don't have to let him off the hook. I'm sure your daughter was upset, and I feel bad about that. Anyway, we'll replace them, but I need to know about where you bought them, and I also need to ask your patience, because, since I don't have a car, it might take me a couple of days to find a ride there."

"I got them at the Walmart in State College. If you want to just repay me—" Her voice trails off rather delicately.

It is hard to judge what strangers might know about me. Among my friends in town I am somewhat famous, the object of teasing for the elaborate lengths I have to go to, to perform some very simple transactions. The fact, however, that they needle me ("Dear Bob, We are having a potluck this Friday. You and Liz and Tommy are invited. Let us know next week, as early as possible, why you didn't come. Love, the Herberts") shows that my habits entertain more than annoy them. A lot goes unspoken, and most of what goes unspoken is about money. I never have to say, as I say to Dr. Harris, "Well, actually, all I have at the moment is about ten dollars, but I should be getting more by the end of the week"—and, in a rush—"actually, I was going to ask you what you paid for them, so I would know how much money to get and take with me."

She is shocked, so she doesn't know anything about me. I fill in quickly, "It's not how it sounds. This is not a hardship, believe me, food out of the babies' mouths or anything like that. I just don't collect money. I get almost everything by barter. Someday I'll tell you about it. But I don't want Annabel to have to be without her dolls."

"They were thirteen apiece."

"Fine. I'll try to have Tommy bring them to her next week."

"Fine. Mr. Miller, I feel like—"

I put my finger to my lips. "Don't say it. The fact is, I live in a weird way and I make people feel funny. But the most important thing is that Tom live through the consequences of those moments when he was breaking the dolls. If you make it easier for me, that will make it easier for him. It can't be easy for him, or he won't learn the real lesson."

"That's true."

"Thanks." We have backed toward the door. She reaches behind me to open it, and I glance around one last time, with the sensation of looking into a Russian Easter egg— the scene, bejeweled with light, is impossibly lovely and self-contained, impossibly unattainable. Her hand on the figured brass doorknob is slim, strong, beautifully manicured, a hand, I realize, that is unlike any hand I've looked at in years, right beneath my gaze, but as far away as a hand in a magazine advertisement. I am disconcerted; then I am on the porch. It is cold and I pull up the hood of my sweat-shirt. The hood string broke long ago, and to replace it, Liz crocheted one from some yarn she'd spun. She hung tassels from it. Tying them fills me with longing for her, and I hunch my shoulders and hurry down the porch steps.

The next four days constitute an orderly demonstration to Tommy of the consequences of his actions. When Martin Summerbee stops by for a visit, I sell him part of the lamb for $26.50. Tommy is standing there. I take him with me when I walk into town on Saturday, looking for a ride to State College, and he watches while I promise a friend of Liz's, Dinah Hart, to till her flower beds one morning in May. "Tom will help," I say. We wait on the porch without speaking while she gets ready to go. The "Jem" dolls are at the far end of the Walmart toy department, requiring a longing march through all the aisles of Transformers, games, art supplies, Legos. He reacts to it all in little starts of recognition, probably with much the same enchantment that I felt in Dr. Harris's lamp-bejeweled front hall. In the doll section, "Kimber" and "Jem" are right on the top, anticlimactic in every way, an obvious waste of money, of effort, of the lambs and the affection and care they repre-sented. I say, "I'm sorry that we have to spend our money on these dolls, Tommy. If you hadn't broken Annabel's, we wouldn't have to."

"I know," he says, chastened, and after that I don't save him by hastening him to the checkout and out the door. I let him look, but not touch. This might have backfired. When we are standing in the vestibule waiting for Dinah, he mutters, "We wouldn't have bought anything, anyway."

I am calm, paternal. I kneel and turn him toward me. His hair is dark brown and springy, his eyes round and thickly lashed. Though he is lanky and slender, his cheeks are round and cherubic. He looks at me, I search his face, and I find no defiance. I say, "Tom, having money and spending money or not is our choice, but wasting it takes our choice away. Do you realize that?"

"Yes, Daddy."

And then Dinah pulls up and I have to believe him. On Monday he takes the dolls to school, and around the place he is helpful and interested, same as always. On Wednesday he brings home another note, this on a half-sheet of peach-colored stationery engraved, "Lydia Martin Harris." It reads,

Dear Mr. and Mrs. Miller,

Annabel is very pleased with the dolls. Thank you for taking such good care of her. Incidents such as this can easily become disasters. It was your prompt and responsible reaction that prevented that in this case. I am new in Moreton, but I hope you will consider me a friend.

Yours truly,
Lydia Harris

And I do. That night the air is especially clear, and when Liz is looking down the valley at Moreton, she says, "Can you pick out the house?"

It takes us a while, and at first we think not—it is hidden by the flank of Snowy Top. But no; Laurel Creek Road curves around the mountain a ways after the Harris place. It is there, its lights seeming to flicker as the breeze tosses about the leafless branches in front of the house. After we find it, Liz says, "Fanlight above the door, you say?"

"Sidelights, too. Even curved windows aren't hard to frame up, you know."

"Ooooh." Liz says. "Mmmm. Let's."

"Miller takeover bid?"

"Miller Conglomerate Expands Holdings Once Again."

3. ❧ November

On the Monday before Thanksgiving, I come into the kitchen for lunch, and Liz tells me that she has been saved. She is smiling, her eyes are sparkling, she looks very flushed and attractive, and so I believe her. After a few moments of confusion, I sit down at the table. I don't know whether to pick up one of my library books from the shelf beside the table, whether to wait for my lunch, or whether to go back out to the barn for a while. I do not, right this minute, want to hear about the circumstances of her salvation, but I am not surprised. Maybe a cancer diagnosis is like this— mortality is expected, but the date comes as a shock.

When I was in the army, I had a buddy named Larry Strunk. We were inducted the same day, trained in the same boot camp, given the same job, and sent to the same unit. For a while we shared the same hooch, and a few times we went on patrol together. In our own minds, our fates became superstitiously entwined, and we even called ourselves "the brothers," only half facetiously. He went out one day and lost his left leg in a mine explosion. Afterward one of my regrets was that we had dared fate by twinning ourselves, however innocently, however jokingly, that we had doomed ourselves to divergence by naming aloud the coincidences and similarities, and feelings of affection that had

"Miller Fanlight Has Wall Street Worried—Can Millers Be Stopped?"

Liz gives a peal of laughter and rolls back on the bed, her feet in the air. "Ha!" she says. "We are so greedy. People don't know how greedy we are." She takes off her overalls, and the moonlight through the window lays a flat, pearly triangle over her thigh, attaching it to the quilt, so that all I want to do is burrow into layers and layers of comfort and warmth and strength and softness. "Come on," she whispers, "come on."

been felt but could have gone unspoken. When I married Liz, I recognized the same magic at work. Now, at the table, it seems to me that she has taken off the way he did, leaving me alone with the old, good life. Certainly she doesn't see it that way.

She says, "I made sweet-potato soup, and there's sprout bread and cream cheese. I'm starving. It looks delicious."

"I want to ask you, but right now wanting to ask you feels sort of like wanting to ask you for all the sexual details of some love affair. Can I wait to ask you until I feel more friendly about it?"

"I would like to tell you."

She speaks simply, with such pure desire to communicate that my heart constricts. We have had great luck in finding one another; we have few conflicts and much pleasure in our friendship; we have been held securely in this bowl of a valley; how can I deny her? I say, "Okay. The moment itself. Make me see the moment itself."

"I was chopping sweet potatoes and looking down the valley. The fog was sort of caught halfway up the mountainsides, as if tangled in the branches, and then it lifted off in big scarves, and the sun shone on the tree branches, and I saw the shapes of the trees, one right after another. Well, the outline of the lower branches exactly matched this imaginary line created along the tips of the upper branches, and it was beautiful and uniform—all the trees were like that. And I thought, The roots are like that, too. Then I thought, Why shouldn't all that striving be toward God's love? Why shouldn't it be God's love that makes it beautiful? The whole history of culture tells us that it IS God's love. Why not just accept it, believe it? Why not? It seemed easy. So I did. It was."

"Sweetie, the world is beautiful. It's beautiful because it and our eyes have evolved together."

"I still believe in Evolution."

"Can't you not be saved? Can't you just believe in God and everything and not be saved?"

"But it feels like being saved. I feel full of relief."

I eat my soup. I could say what I feel, "Don't leave me," but she would think I meant something practical. I know she won't leave the farm, our marriage. I know, in fact, that this latest event represents the completion of that circle to her. I have been in love with Liz for twelve years, and our love grew largely out of shared interests, ideas, and ambitions. We have disagreed and compromised and learned from one another, and one of the things I love most about her is how she suggests new possibilities to me after the moment of anger as if they were speculations rather than issues. She is respectful of everyone, including Tom, including me. She makes it easy to learn from her. But being saved religiously is not something I want to learn, that is in me to learn. Nor, I suspect, is it something learnable, but, rather, a native talent. I could probably learn the formalities, but I could never make the leap of faith. Liz won't see it neutrally, like this; she will certainly move willy-nilly toward giving that talent a moral color, using words like "choice," "commitment," "good," "necessary." Her "Bright Light" church doesn't admit enough room for compromise, if any form of Christianity does.

She scarfs down her soup and two or three pieces of bread, not really more lustily than usual—she is a passionate eater most of the time. Then she sits back and says, "Bobby, this is good news."

"On what plane?"

She smiles merrily. "How about the every-little-sparrow-that-falls plane?"

"God is happy?"

"I think so. I think he's happy but not elated, sort of the way you are when you plant lettuce seeds and they sprout, rather than as you would be if you planted lemon trees in

Pennsylvania and they bore fruit. I don't imagine it's a miracle for him."

"Is it a miracle for you?"

She gets up from her seat and plunks herself in my lap. "Only for me. It feels very private. I like it that way. Nothing is going to change. It makes me love you more."

Well, it is easy to notice the foolishness of the transported, the sorts of promises they make, their unwillingness to admit the practical cost soon to be paid, their self-confidence. So let me not notice it, as Liz has not rolled her eyes in the past at my "great ideas." Let us stay married, nuzzling, agreeing, eating, talking, being all the more present now that we recognize transience in a new way.

On Wednesday morning I go for the turkey. The fact is, I've gotten one every year so far, though more than once it's taken from sunup to sunset. Turkeys are easier to hunt in the spring, when they are mating. You can go out before dawn and find them roosting in the trees, silhouetted against the lightening sky, and you can call them down to you at daybreak with a hen call, and often the tom will come at a run. In the fall their desires are more discreet—food and friendship—and they are far more suspicious. You have to call infrequently, no more than two or three times an hour, and, I always think, your call has to sound rather casual, relaxed but informative, as if the turkey you are is offering good conversation about safe and pleasant topics. You also have to stay as still as possible, since their hearing is exceptional and their eyesight is better than that. With all your efforts, a turkey in the fall still approaches mistrustfully, a step at a time, so you have time to debate over and over about whether it is in range or not, whether you are a decent shot or not, whether you've been kidding yourself all year about your marksmanship, whether you have also been kidding yourself about lots of other things, whether now is the time to give up meat-eating, whether you are cold and uncomfortable enough to go home—but still you are riveted, can't move, enthralled by your power over the turkey.

A flock has included the back part of our woods in its range this year: I have seen tracks and feeding signs all summer. I intend to outsmart the birds this year, and not to spend as much time as usual doing it. At the breakfast table, Tommy says, "Hey, Daddy, aren't you going to get a turkey this year?"

"It'll be here when you get home from school." I sound lordly.

He looks around the room. "You said you've to jump them when they're still sleepy."

"That's the spring. Don't worry. I've got those turkeys all figured out this year."

"Famous last words," remarks Liz.

"Keep talking. We'll see."

Liz laughs. "How about a nice turkey breast molded out of mashed turnips? Mmm."

"I want turkey!"

"And there is a turkey who wants you. You watch. Now, here, how many shells do I have in my hand?"

"Three."

"That's all I'm taking. One to scatter the flock, one to kill the dinner bird, and one to fiddle with in my pocket for good luck."

He picks up one of the shells. They are my last three from a box I bought four years ago. I say, "Better still, you keep that for good luck all day at school."

"Good luck if you want cream cheese for Thanksgiving dinner," snorts Liz.

Tommy is grinning as he slips the shell into his breast pocket. I say, "Now don't show it to anyone. Otherwise the luck will run out of it, and we won't have turkey for Thanksgiving. Got that?"

"Yeah. Yeah, I guess."

"It's our secret? Promise?"

"Promise."

"Two-shot-turkey promise?"

"Yeah."

"The look" passes over him; he clenches his palm and one or two breaths come suddenly and fast, but he is good—he puckers and blows off the extra energy, waits a second, and then goes back to eating his toast. I feel as if I have just witnessed a private ritual exorcism, and I don't want to lay claim to it by mentioning it, so after a little bit I say, "It'll be great. I'll be thinking of you, son."

The trees are hung with mist, and the cloud cover is low enough to shroud the upper ridges—a good day for hunting, since the damp leaves under my feet make little noise as I climb the hill behind the house. At "the deer clearing" (a spot where we used to see deer once or twice a week), I pause, as I always do, and look over the roof of the house, down the valley. The roof of the house is blackly wet, mostly hidden in a tangle of branches. Our gardens, fenced, covered with leaves, make a neat pattern, attentive to the house, like seats in an amphitheater. Moreton is hidden in thick mist. It would be an ugly day anywhere else, but here it is only a particular kind of day, autumnal and interior. It feels adventurous to be out.

I check the springhouse and the water pipe. The clear, still water, dark in the shady springhouse tank, is about three feet deep. A steady trickle of water flows into it from above—rather than using a pipe, I took a chisel, and chiseled a deep conduit in a flat piece of sandstone that was already in place. I thought it was an especially tactful way of capping the spring. From the tank, buried pipe runs to the pump by the sink in the house. Buried four feet deep. The trench took Martin Summerbee and me a summer to dig, but it has never frozen up, even in the coldest winter. The spring produces about a gallon a minute, even in the summer, and gives me the secret security of buried treasure—when I bought the land, I thought I would use the old well, but I discovered the first summer that its lower reaches were caved in and that digging a new well, if the driller could even get in to the house, would run about a thousand dollars—eight hundred more than I had. It was the well-driller who said he'd heard there were springs all over this ridge. The fact is, I used to think that the pleasure of receiving the earth's free gifts—water, raspberries, firewood, walnuts—would fade with habit, but it hasn't. That's another prayer—good luck that feels like gratitude.

I cross the ridge onto the neighboring property, and encounter turkey sign almost immediately. It is not only tracks, but also the shadowy, rounded shapes in the dirt that they make with their wattles as they forage. I put the call to my mouth and give two quiet "cluck"s. A turkey answers almost immediately, from a cleft not far below me, where I happen to know that a spring rises and a clearing spreads in a gentle slope toward an old deer-blind. Between me and the clearing is a heavy thicket of young sugar maples and yellow birch. A turkey won't enter a thicket, so I can use it as a blind from which to look down at the spring. I load one of the shells, take the safety off, and glide toward the thicket.

The turkeys are feeding in a group near the spring, the tom, three hens, and two young birds. When I stretch out on a big flat rock and give a single cluck, the two young birds come toward me at once, five or six steps. The nearest hen looks up curiously, too. She is my target, a twelve- or thirteen-pound bird, probably not very old. I take aim. She continues to look around. Through the sights she seems larger, and seems to take on personality. I choose her, as if I were choosing the smartest, most alert puppy from a litter. I squeeze the trigger, willing myself to resist the recoil and the noise of the shot.

jumping up and shouting, "Surprise!" but I restrain her, and we keep watching. He stands back then and gazes at the turkey, arms crossed over his chest. He gazes for a long time, much longer than I would have thought possible for him. This is a fidgety kid, one who can hardly stand to read for half an hour in his room, who has to be asked to sit down at the table over and over during a meal. Now, though, he seems to be drinking this turkey in. No toe-tapping, head-scratching, sniffling. Nothing. When I become impatient, Liz restrains me. And then he steps forward and strokes the turkey's breast with the back of his hand, gently, three times. He reaches toward the turkey's head. We can't stand it any longer—neither of us—we spring up and yell, "Surprise!" He jumps back, laughs, becomes a son again, says, "Daddy! You got it!"

I take the remaining shell out of my shirt pocket. "One shot," I say.

"Wow!" he says, and we have a romantic night that night, all enamored of one another, of our house, our coming feast, of the beneficent turkey spirit that seems to have come for a visit.

The day after Thanksgiving, we walk into town for supper at the Claytons' house. It is a yearly ritual—we walk to town, eat early, and all go to a movie in State College. This year we consider seeing *Platoon*. It is my decision, since I am the only veteran, but confronting my war experiences is not something I want to do on my one night out for the year, and we go to *Radio Days* instead. Dr. Harris is standing in line ahead of us. I can't tell if she is alone or with the group just in front of her. She is wearing a thick, stylish camel's hair coat, a fur hat, and leather gloves. I wave, and, after a moment, she waves. I wonder if our behavior would be different if we were going to be friends.

Then, on the last day of November, just after lunch, I

By the time the thunder has dissipated, the turkeys have scattered into the woods, nowhere to be seen. In a heap of feathers near the spring lies not the little hen but the tom himself, who must have walked into the shot, which I must have misjudged because I was shooting downhill. I have never felt a sense of triumph at actually bagging the game, rather a kind of panic at having to approach it, touch it. There is a heart-sinking moment like exhaustion when I think of all the work ahead of me: gutting, dressing, trudging home, singeing, cooking, even eating, and wish I were still in that happy, unencumbered previctorious state.

It is carrying the bird home through the trees, tromping through the leaves, surveying the landscape that brings me back to myself. And, of course, Liz is impressed. It isn't even lunchtime yet, and this is the biggest turkey I've ever shot.

At three-thirty, we hear the school bus gear up as it pulls away from dropping Tommy at the end of the road. We have left the feathers on the turkey for just this moment. Liz hastily spreads the wings on newspapers on the front porch, to display them, and we hide inside the kitchen door. The turkey seems about six feet long, so large that it is nearly human in some way. I can't resist peering out and spying on my son's progress toward the house—it is a weakness I have always had for wanting to know the solitary, undefended Tom. At first his step is idle—he drops his coat, steps on it by mistake, hastily picks it up and brushes at the dirt. Then he makes himself be more careful. At last he decides to run. About ten feet in front of the porch he stops short, startled and, maybe, afraid for a moment. He cranes his neck to get a better look at the turkey, realizes what it is, and climbs the steps. His awe is everything I could have asked for. "Wow," he says. "It's the turkey." He walks all the way around it, fingers some of the wing feathers, pokes the beak, picks up one of the feet. I can feel Liz tense for

hear a car turn into our road and stop. The slam of the door rings out in the clear, cold air. I am in my woodshop, weaving chair seats. I continue to weave for a bit, then look up to see Liz standing on the front porch, wiping her hands. She is alert, still. After a long moment, I realize that I, too, have been sitting without moving, without looking around to see who is coming, only gripping the chair and the cane, tightly.

It is Dr. Harris. Liz strides out to meet her, and as I come up to them, she is saying, "The post office told me how to get here. I would have called ahead—"

"It's fine," says Liz. "Really. Won't you come in?"

"No." She starts fumbling with a bag she is carrying, and I feel myself staring at her hands. She says, "The school called me at the university and I thought I'd better—" Smiles flit uncomfortably across her face. She brings forth a lavender child's coat, new and pretty. Someone has taken a scissors and cut it up the back in jagged strokes almost to the collar. "Apparently he took the scissors out of the teacher's desk during recess—"

"Tommy did? Tommy cut this coat during recess?" Liz's voice is shaking.

"No. Yes. I mean, no, she was wearing it during recess, but that's when he took the scissors. He cut it in the cloakroom during personal reading time."

"Are you sure? Is the teacher sure it was Tommy? I got the impression that she was sort of predisposed against—"

"Some other children were watching him. He asked them to watch him."

What I am aware of is the color of her face, how its strangeness makes what she is saying totally incomprehensible to me. Recess, cloakroom, personal reading time. These seem like foreign words, communicating nothing, and yet the sight of it unfolds within me as she speaks—

Tommy with "the look," excited at the attention of the others, struggling to force the unwieldy shears through the thick cloth, giving off that sense of awkward muscular tension Liz and I are both familiar with. I know what she says is true, but she has become so important and strange telling me about it, then standing here, gazing at me, that I have no response.

Liz says, "Please come in and have some tea or something." Not an offer, but a plea. Lydia Harris acquiesces.

She doesn't fit into our house. There is a finish to her clothing, her shoes, her skin that looks in danger of being snagged on the rough surfaces that we live with—brick, cane, wood—and she hesitates before laying her camel's hair coat over the arm of my Windsor chair. No one says anything until Liz puts her hand on the kettle, and then, given courage, I suppose, by familiarity, she says, "Robert tells me you're a doctor at the university."

"I teach in the math department. This is my first year."

"Where were you before?"

"Boston. Before that, Berkeley. My husband teaches at Harvard. I was filling in at Boston, uh, University, and then I got this job, which is a real job, so I took it. I was raised in the country, so it was tempting to try that again."

"That's interesting."

She looks around, somewhat furtively, her glance lingering over the twelve-drawer chest on chest and the two corner cupboards. If we were going to be friends, I would ask her what she teaches and she would ask where we got such elegant pieces of furniture. Instead, I say, "Obviously, we're appalled that Tommy has done this. I mean—"

Liz interrupts, "It's not just that he's destroyed something—"

"It's more that he must have hurt your daughter. It's so aggressive—"

Liz interrupts again. "It's so jagged. I hate that part of

it." She smiles sadly. "It was a pretty coat, too. I love that color."

"It was new. I mean, maybe that's the key. The things he damages are Annie's new things. I asked her if he was mean to her, or if the other kids were, and she said not. Even so, I'm not sure she's been entirely accepted by the other children. Sometimes it takes a while with children of color, especially in a rural setting, and I told her about that, and to expect that. We've talked lots of times about what goes on at school, and how she might look at it. I don't know. I was raised in Tennessee. Part of me says that if it isn't terrifying, then it's okay."

Liz says, "Isn't this terrifying?"

Lydia Harris gives a knowing smile. "Terrifying is when the parents are the source of the trouble, not the kids." She looks me in the eye. "I admit I was suspicious at first. I always am. But right now it doesn't seem like you all condone Tom's behavior, so I'm sure he'll get over it. I do have faith that if we keep in touch, we can contain this."

At last I can speak. "We'd better. I will, too."

She looks in her cup, takes another sip, then stands to go. She looks once again around the room, and I know she is thinking about money. She says, "I can afford to replace the coat."

"I can't afford to let you."

"It was sixty-five dollars."

"When I work for people in town, I charge seven-fifty an hour. Find me ten hours of work around your house. It's an old house, and I can do anything. I built this furniture. I built this house. You won't be making do."

She runs her hand over the scrolling of the chest on chest.

"Black walnut. Used to stand over by the barn."

"He can make anything," says Liz.

"I'll think about it," says Dr. Harris. "All the stories say you have to think carefully if you are going to make a wish."

She doesn't smile, does gather her belongings, refuses to have me walk her to her car. After she leaves, Liz and I sit dumbfounded at the table.

When I was about nine, my father gave me the free run of the town we lived in. As long as I was home for dinner, I could ride my bike anywhere I wanted to. I was still sort of out of control, and I think he pictured me spreading my energy over a wider area, and therefore getting into less trouble. I had two friends, and we used to bike out to the development at the edge of town and play in the new houses. There were other kids, boys and girls, we played with in the development, and one day, when we were exploring the neighborhood, we found an old Dodge pickup parked on a sloping driveway above a cornfield. One of the other kids got in and let out the parking brake, and the rest of us rolled it back into the cornfield. We all took turns sitting behind the wheel, beeping the horn, and shifting the gears; then we started throwing clods of dirt at the windows and mirrors. We broke them all, then threw more clods of dirt through the holes. At dinnertime we went home. We didn't talk about it, and I'm pretty sure I didn't think about it again for a month, maybe. But later in the spring, late enough so that all the windows and doors in the house were open, I remember that I was watching TV after school and a shadow fell through the screen door across the living-room carpet, and I knew without looking up that I was in trouble about that truck.

My mother answered the door, and I looked up. It was a policeman. The truck, we were told, had been worth four hundred dollars. My share was a hundred. I worked almost the whole of the next year, at a dollar an hour, to repay my father for what he paid the owner of the truck. I was also spanked, lectured, and sent to my room. But the real moment of punishment, of dread to the point of physical pain,

there are none. The future is no mystery to him. Still, he doesn't pause or slow down, and in spite of myself I rather love the bravery in his straight, deliberate course. He climbs the porch steps and knocks at the kitchen door. Liz's arm appears; he disappears. As per her instructions, I weave an entire chair seat before leaving the barn. There is plenty of time for me to contemplate how fatherhood has made an actor of me, and a good one. As with any role, it has given me new feelings to feel as well as to express, and when I am preparing for one of fatherhood's dramatic moments, as I am now, I always have a sliding sensation. The lines I think of rev me up, and the impending assumption of righteousness seems both alluring and scary. By the time I have tied off the rushes and latched the barn door, it is nearly dark.

At first it looks like they are simply sitting quietly at the table, but then I realize that they are praying. In the Bright Light church, various postures are required for various attitudes of prayer, which has always made me suspect that the prophet tarried for a time among the religions of the East. The sitting attitude is a contemplative one—the supplicant asks to be shown the inner workings of his or her soul. It has the advantage of being unobtrusive anywhere, and therefore appropriate anytime the believer has an idle moment. If the believer is then moved to adopt an "attack" posture (my term), the sitting posture gives him time to prepare for it. Oh, yes. They are praying. Every event around the house has taken on so many new layers it is only possible to begin with a question.

"Son, did you know whose coat you were cutting?"

"Yes, Daddy."

"Did you set out to cut it a long time ago, or only just today?"

"I don't know. I thought about it more today."

was my first glimpse of that policeman through the screen door.

At last I say to Liz, "We should have had her leave the coat. Then we could have just set it on the table to speak for itself."

"I don't think he did it. I can't imagine it."

"I can. He did."

"You can imagine your own son plotting to take the scissors out of the teacher's desk, then recruiting other kids to watch, then destroying something like that?"

"I can imagine any boy doing it. I can imagine myself doing it."

"I'm sure he didn't do it."

"Liz—"

"Something else happened."

"Are you saying they're all lying?"

"If I have to."

"Lizzie—"

"Why do you trust strangers before your own son?"

I get up to go to her, but she turns abruptly toward the sink. "Just don't yell at him first. Just let's ask him first."

"You're not being—"

"And don't lie in wait for him. Let him come in and eat his snack first."

"Elizabeth—"

She spins toward me. "You know what? When I saw that coat, I wanted to have it! I wanted to be seven years old again, and to be wearing that darling coat to school every day. I just yearned for it. That's a color that never turns up at the Goodwill."

I go out into my shop and sit down on one of my chairs. A while later Tom trudges past, and when he casts a glance toward the barn, I press myself away from the window, so he won't see me. I am eagle-eyed for signs of frivolity, but

4. ❧ January

I spend two days at Lydia Harris's house, stripping and refinishing woodwork in the dining room. There are only two coats of paint. The work is easy and the results surprising—the wood is local butternut, pale and smooth, almost white; it doesn't quite go with the oak flooring, which is probably why it was painted, and yet it is unusual and pleasing. Lydia stands in the middle of the room, trying to decide from color cards what shade to finish it in, and says, "I feel like I just splurged on a wonderful new pair of shoes, and now I have to buy a whole new wardrobe to go with it." The husband, whose name is Nathan, has gone back to Harvard. I say, "Maybe your husband will have some suggestions."

Lydia laughs, "Oh, Nathan! He doesn't care. He says paint everything white enamel and hose it down. He did the wiring, though, before we moved in. He's very mechanical, for a mathematician."

Tom and Annabel are back in school. I clear my throat and wait, trying to find a comfortable way to stand: the floor is not level, I can sense it if I'm not distracted by work, and it makes me edgy. There are other things about the house that make me uneasy. The air moves a lot, so that I can feel it rolling around my neck and shoulders. On the second floor, paint is peeling off the chimney wall, showing that water vapor and maybe fumes are leaking through the chimney tiles. The mullioned windows have no storms, and are frosted on the inside. There is plenty of work here, but I don't want to do it. I plan to mention these things sometime, after I have lost my identity as a handy sort of person.

"Let's do this," she says. "Let's paint the wall below the molding a silvery green, which will bleach out both the floor and the rest of the woodwork. Then, above the moldings, I'll paper with something rosy, which will draw the eye upward. So go ahead, leave it pale. It's just too unusual to cover up. The table doesn't matter. I'll get a new table."

I begin brushing on tung oil, and after a while she joins me. Like Liz, she is the sort of woman who works steadily without saying much, and she is orderly and neat. I forget she is here until she says, "I've thought a lot about those beautiful pieces you have at your place. The dark walnut chest is one of the loveliest things I've ever seen. What did you stain it with?"

"I soaked crushed walnut husks in alcohol."

"Would you sell it?"

"It belongs to my wife."

Silence; then, "I envy you your talents."

"I envy you your colors."

"Pardon me?"

"The colors. The way you imagine colors together. When you were talking about how you were going to paint the room, it pleased me just to hear about it. I was impressed, too, at how quickly you saw the whole, and how you didn't just solve the problem, but made something out of it. Liz and I love our life, but it's funny how we miss color."

Stroke. Stroke. I like the way work relieves conversation of duty, supplies it with time to ponder what has been said. I expect Lydia to ask me about our life, but instead I ask about hers: "What sort of math do you teach?"

tential, contract cancer or heart disease? My grandfather was untouched by these issues—they were quirks of fate or nature, fixed elements of identity, more than anything ways to differentiate among the members of a group. He did not think of problems as effects he might have caused, more as afflictions. After raising many dogs and rearing many sons, he took on an air of solid completeness, squared off, gracious. He said, "Your sons weren't made to like you. That's what grandchildren are for."

So, for today, let me take refuge in his clarity. Let me, for the moment, not see with the eyes that the last half of the twentieth century has given me, eyes that pick out the tiny, glinting threads of cause and effect running everywhere, eyes that automatically superimpose the past boy upon the present man, the future man upon the present boy. I am cool and resolved. I spell out moral values, expectations, and consequences. I punish and promise more punishment. I make sure he understands. I assert authority. I bring things to that impossible point, an end.

"Did you ask the other kids to watch you, or did they just watch you?"

"I asked a couple."

"Why did you want them to watch you?"

"I don't know."

"Why did you cut the coat?"

"I don't know."

"Did you enjoy doing it?"

"I don't know."

"Don't you like Annabel?"

"She's okay."

"Then why hurt her this way? Does she provoke you?"

"What?

"Does she say mean things to you or about you?"

"I don't know."

As we are having this discussion, Liz lights the kerosene lamps and sets the casserole of beans and rice in the range. Its fragrance, compounded of coriander seed and dill seed, floats around us. His answers are hypnotic: cause and effect seem to part from one another, promising that to seek any further into the sources of these events will yield nothing. The key now is to simply act, to act simply—to forbid, to punish, to exact payment, to make sure he is listening, that he understands. My grandfather, who had five sons and many dogs, always swore he treated boys and Saint Bernards the same way. He convinced them when they were small that he was bigger and knew more than they did. Even when they outweighed him and had more schooling, they were so in the habit of obedience that he didn't have any trouble. My father and his brothers all had jobs and families whom they supported. This was the fundamental test of my grandfather's method. Were they happy? Did they drink, harbor extreme political views, display long-standing anger, treat their wives well, live up to their po-

And maybe she sat up last night, unseeing among all the glittering lights and colors, and speculated about Liz and me. Mutual fascination is as possible as mutual friendship or a mutually satisfactory business arrangement, isn't it?

When I invite her to bring Annabel and go skating sometime, she jumps at the chance.

After I am finished, I choose to ski home over the fields rather than take a ride. The snow is deep and crusty, and all day long I have been promising myself these cool monochromes. On the way through town, I pass a number of good friends, people whose company, rooms, dinner tables, and conversation have given me great pleasure, but I make excuses to hurry. The fact is, more talk with Lydia Harris keeps unrolling in my head. There is nothing I don't want to know about her, nothing I don't want her to know about me. It feels like lust, agitating and restless, but it is not that. It is more like some judgment that I seek, on the worth of my very nature.

As I work for Lydia, so Tom works for me, to reimburse my labor of paying for the lavender coat. Plan A was to have him in her house, helping me under the very eyes of Annabel Harris, but they didn't want the place torn up during the holidays, and of course Tom must go to school. Plan B involves twenty hours of extra effort at three dollars an hour. Tom goes about his work without complaining, about an hour a day. He is on hour seven. He must keep a record of the hours and of his tasks, so that he can know what the coat cost him. Supervising this work, I am sober and demanding. When the work ends, I always relax and provide some treat. I shouldn't, but I can't resist.

Today he is washing windows—only the insides, since the weather is cold—and I sit with him while he does it. I try to meet his chatter with cool silence. He says, "Daddy, do you think Sparkle is going to get to fourteen hands?"

"I don't know. Maybe. Don't count on it."

"Fourteen hands is big for a pony. Over fourteen hands, it's a little horse."

"Don't forget that corner."

"Don't you like Sparkle's white feet? Her white socks. They don't go above the pastern joint, so they aren't stockings. That's my favorite part about her."

"Why don't you rinse out your rag now? It's getting a little dirty."

"I think Sparkle is a very pretty pony. She has a good head, better than Henrietta's. Do you think Mr. Halloran would let us breed to his stallion again? He's a good stud. We could raise lots of ponies and train them and sell them, and give Mr. Halloran half the money."

"I want you to go right along the putty there, and get that dust off. That's from the woodstove, and it could eat into the woodwork eventually."

"I love Sparkle. She's really smart, Daddy. I had this carrot for her, and I was keeping it in my pocket, and she found it right away and put her nose into my pocket, but she was really careful and didn't tear the pocket or anything."

"Sparkle is a good pony."

"I'm glad she's a filly, because then, when she grows up, she can have foals, too. Can we build a cart and teach Sparkle to pull it? I bet, if we let her run around, she would stay close to the house, and then she could come to my window and put her head in and wake me up in the morning."

"Son, she's not a dog."

"But she's really smart, Daddy. She knows me, and she likes me, because I know just where to scratch her and stuff."

"How was school?"

"Okay. I wish we could go skating."

School is not something he talks about, but he didn't talk about it last year, either. When he finishes the windows, I see that he has done a good job, not only careful. I don't compliment him or thank him, but get up deliberately and go out to milk the goats without inviting him along. After dinner, though, apropos of nothing, I suggest that we go skating in the moonlight, all together.

The pond is hidden from the house by trees, another scenic mistake I would have avoided had I sited the house properly. It is a biggish pond, though, almost an acre, fed by a little stream. It was dammed a hundred years ago at least, and they did such a good job that all I have had to do is replace a few stones from time to time. The night is moonless and starry, cold and still. There has been no snow since we last skated, so the ice is clear, fluorescent. Impatient, Tom skates away from us, backward, awkward but determined. This is something he has just learned this year. I watch Liz put on her white figure skates. She pulls the strings tight, ties them carefully, businesslike, but then she leans back and points her toes, as if the skates were ballet slippers, and admires them. She is the skater of us all, having taken lessons as a child. Our skates are good ones, have lasted since our marriage. Her mother was going to give us china and linens. We asked for skates as if we were taking a political position, so she gave us custom-made Canadian skates. Her revenge was that we had to go to the sports store for three separate fittings.

On skates, Liz is not immediately transformed. Her flat-footed personality clings at first—her overalls are baggy, her old down coat makes her thick and matter-of-fact, she keeps her hands in her pockets. She cuts across the pond four times, picking up twigs and other trash. She tempts me to stop watching her, but I don't. I might miss the moment when her arms spread, her head turns, and she suddenly slips into a big backward circle, lazy but sharp, her body as silver and definite as a trout's. Then she is moving backward on one leg, the other leg straight behind her, toe pointed. Her head is flat, turned, her arms flung beyond her head. An invisible thread looped through her outstretched skate seems to be towing her across the ice. She finishes with a spin, and her hat flies off. Tom retrieves it and returns it to her. They embrace, and she takes his hand and twirls him around. He stumbles but keeps his feet, laughing.

Now it is my turn. I haven't mastered much, but I can go fast, and the acre of the pond is hardly big enough to contain me when I am really in the mood. I begin by drifting around the edge, getting the feel of the ice, of my skates, of my legs and lower back, stroking, gliding, crossing into a turn. It is soothing and stimulating at the same time, so easy that I am tempted, as always, to go off into my own arabesque and triple jump. There is no reason why not. The body is willing, tingles with anticipation. Except that the readiness is an illusion, and all I have ever done is to go forward, fast, and backward, slowly. I make myself settle down. In the middle of the pond, Tommy is practicing, staring at his feet. I skate a circle around him.

"What are you trying to do, son?"

"There's a way you can turn your skates to stop so that they shoot some snow into the air. Mommy can do it."

"Don't you have to be going pretty fast?"

"I'm going fast."

I skate away in a big loop and return, orbit him, and skate away again. Across the pond, Liz is cutting figure eights, trying to track the same circles over and over again. Tommy continues to flail through a few big strides, slide, and then stop. He never falls, but he never looks like he is skating, either, more like he is leaping though shallow surf. I skate another ring around him, and then the phrase comes to me, "running rings around him." I wonder if it's possible, especially if he had some direction across the pond and no reason to limit his speed. I loop him again, this time orbiting like a planet instead of a comet, Mars, say. Earth. Venus. "Hey, watch out," he shouts. Back to Mars. Out to Jupiter, so that he doesn't get self-conscious. It is a strange and exhilarating feeling, circling him like this, sort of stroboscopic. The pleasure is watching his intensity revealed sequentially—in his face, his taut left arm, the arc of his shoulders, his right hip, his back again. I can even trick myself into thinking I am stationary and he is doing a slow, impossible spin here in the glinting blue darkness. I am a camera. I am a fence, a palisade, a moat, enclosing him. Now he looks up and sighs, glances at me, and begins to skate away. The real test. I turn and skate after him, one loop: I make a silly face, he laughs. Around his back, then another loop—they have to be tight, which slows me down, makes them harder. I throw my arms out, stick out my tongue. He laughs again, then speeds up. Now I am almost chasing him, the hare after the tortoise. He heads for his mother. The distance between them begins to close up. I put on speed, flatten my ring, go straight at them. "Hey, Mom," he calls. Her arm goes out, oblivious. Between them is a doorway, a window, the eye of a needle. I shoot through it, brushing both of them lightly with the flapping tails of my coat. "Hey!" says Liz. I imagine them falling into one another's arms.

At the end of the pond I turn around, flushed with adrenaline. Tom is showing Liz how he has learned to stop. She is praising him. I would like to skate rings around the two of them, slow, lazy orbits lasting days, a ritual of discreet containment, nothing coercive, no fences in the open pasture, only an alert dog at one end. When we are undressing to get into bed later, Liz says, "That was fun, wasn't it? I think the nice thing about our family is that there's all sorts of fun going around, and it's easy to catch some."

Still later, in the dark, when I am nearly asleep, she says, "Were you skating rings around him?"

"Exactly. Are you reading my mind again?"

"I wish I could. But I hear you have to be married for twenty years for that."

"Maybe we could apply for early access."

"I'll call tomorrow." I can feel her smile in the dark, against the crook of my shoulder. I am very warm.

A brother of Liz's worked for the post office one Christmas, and he said that they were told that, if the truck got stuck, they should get out some fourth-class mail and throw it under the wheels. That's the kind of package we get at the end of the month: dirty pages numbered 6 through 15 in a plastic bag with a fragment of a manila envelope containing only our address and a December 12 postmark. No letter, no return address, no clue of the sender until we begin deciphering the text. It is the chapter of Tina Morrissey's book and begins, "fish bones and heads from the nearby trout stream, as well as sheep and cattle manure, rotted hay and grass clippings, maple and beech leaves, sawdust, wood shavings, wood ash. The five heaps measure about ten feet by ten feet by ten feet, so the Millers have stockpiled some five thousand cubic feet of excellent organic compost. Bob uses it liberally, digging as much as two of the heaps into his beds each year. He has neatly solved the problem of access to such large heaps by building a kind of movable tunnel out of old boards and wheels from two children's wagons. He rolls the tunnel up to the open side of one of the heaps and begins shoveling from the bottom. As he digs his way into the mound, the boards that form the roof of the tunnel support the mound and direct it downward toward the center."

Liz finds this very funny, and for the next hour keeps erupting with barks of laughter. I say, "It's a good idea."

"It's a great idea, but I have this image of you tunneling

into this mountain of shit. Just a little man in a raincoat. Bye, Bob, see you in the spring!"

"You've seen me get compost, and you've gotten it yourself."

"I'm not laughing at you, honey, I'm laughing at the image."

I read the rest by myself, remembering my fears of how she would perceive our family, our likability as personalities. But it does not read, "For a profoundly neurotic son of a bitch, Bob Miller has done pretty well." It reads, "Miller is careful to keep his carrot seeds moist until they germinate. He covers each bed with two layers of old newspapers, and then sprinkles these layers sometimes four or five times a day with water from the spring. After seven days of this treatment, Miller gets almost 100 percent germination, rare for carrot seed, which under normal conditions offers 30–40 percent germination in two to three weeks." About Tom she writes, "Even the seven-year-old is an integral part of the family effort." She calls our valley "a kind of paradise from which the Millers can catch sight of the twentieth century (as it is played out in the supermarket and the branch bank in Moreton, a town of a thousand people) without having to participate in it." Nowhere does she call me a genius, but she does remark that "Miller's manner is not unlike that of some powerful and wealthy CEO. He does what he wants, the way he wants to do it. Surely this comes from rejecting the power of money and from cultivating his ability to grow, build, catch, or find everything he not only needs, but wants." I am not exactly flattered. Maybe there was once a letter, asking my opinion of this, or whether I would like to make changes, but it is gone now, along with the return address. The manuscript pages lie around for a few days, then disappear.

Liz gets up on Sunday and says, "Tom's going to church with me today. We can ski. The snow is good and there isn't any wind, so we shouldn't have any trouble. How would you like pancakes for breakfast?" It's an effective speech, and leaves me perplexed. Any question will be a challenge now. I say, "Pancakes sound good," and leave it at that. Later I plan to try the "I thought we were going to talk about this" line, because I thought we were, even though I don't suppose we agreed on it. We clean up the bedroom and make the bed, waiting to see who will make the next misstep, and finally Liz says, "He asked to go."

"He'll miss pony training."

"He asked me to ask you if you could save that till the afternoon."

"I had other plans for the afternoon."

"Could you be a little flexible?"

"Pony training is in the morning. A regular routine is important, both to the pony and to Tom. The ponies will be standing at the gate, expecting to be trained and fed again. I want to encourage those sorts of habits."

"I understand that—" But she doesn't go on. Over our whole-wheat pancakes and applesauce we talk about planting blue potatoes this year, and blue corn. Tom would like to know if blue tomatoes are available, and I try to explain that blue is somehow genetically related to yellow, but not to red. They exchange occasional looks across the table which I can't read, and I sound pedantic to myself, loud and overly informative. Even so, Tom stays home and Liz skis off by herself.

The pony foal is nearly a year old now—she was born in March—and one or both of us has worked with her every day since she was born. She wears a halter, walks on a lead, and allows all of her feet to be picked up. Her skin twitches when we brush her, and her little tail switches impatiently back and forth. Her winter coat is thick, nearly black, dull in tone. Tom lets her take an apple that he holds between his teeth, and I don't stop him. She is careful—her velvety upper lip stretches and feels the skin of the apple, pulls it away from him almost prehensilely. He is on his best behavior with her; his hands move slowly and firmly over her coat. He stands very close to her and never moves around her without maintaining contact. He speaks in a low, definite voice. The boyish urge to supply cause and witness effect that impels him, sometimes, to blow into the mother pony's ears or sprinkle water on the cats or walk right behind the sheep, so they can hear him but can't see him, is absent with the pony foal. He wants her to be calm and happy and smart and pretty, to love him and obey him and grow up smoothly, as any parent does.

I push open the barn door, and he leads her out into the snow. She walks two steps, then snorts and kicks out with one back foot. He leads her steadily forward, the way I taught him, never looking at her, never acting as though she has done anything out of the ordinary. She tries a little buck and kick, then tries to reach her nose down to the snow. He casts me one glance over his shoulder. He is a little afraid—she is a little friskier than usual, because of the cold. "Keep going," I say. "She's paying attention." I follow them around the corner of the barn and down the long side. At the barnyard fence they stop and turn around and begin back toward me. He is holding her loosely, his right hand next to the leadline clip, the free end of the rope in his left. Every day one of us does this, over this same ground, past these same windows that look in upon the same assortment of livestock, but today, for the first time, the pony foal notices something—a blatting goat? a cat?— and she suddenly jerks away from Tommy, backing and shying, her nostrils wide and her ears bolted forward. He loses her with his right hand, but his left instinctively tightens on the rope and she jerks him around. I can see the look of surprise and panic on his face as she begins to pull him in a circle, throwing her head, bucking, kicking, neighing, now taking offense at every sound and movement in the vicinity.

The smartest thing for him to do would be to let go of the rope, and actually I have never thought to tell him what to do in this sort of circumstance—the mother pony is phlegmatic, and the pony foal has been so cooperative until now that her manners seemed permanent. But he doesn't do the smartest thing; he reacts like a natural horseman and hangs on tight. There would be lots of reasons, if he knew them: to keep her from running off and maybe hurting herself, to keep her from successfully getting her way, to maintain his contact with her and therefore her attention upon him. I don't panic. I don't rush toward them. Whether by instinct, trust, or foolishness, I don't react as if he is in danger, I just watch them float in the black-and-white picture created by trees and snow, yanking, tossing, pulling at each other. He keeps saying, "Sparkle! Sparkle!" His hat falls off. They are pretty far away when I finally begin to run toward them, dilatory father.

When I reach them they are still, if not calm. The pony is trembling and heaving, Tom is panting, his cheeks are aflame. They can barely walk, but I make them. Back to the spot where she shied, back to that moment, so that we can go over it and over it, erasing with habit any associations she might have with that spot. Was he in danger? I don't know, but it is by common, and unvoiced, consent that we don't bother to tell Liz about it when she returns in the afternoon.

That week is bitter cold, and it snows a few inches every day. Books and magazines are due at the library, and we long for new ones, but there is no going anywhere. Tom takes the bus, but we wrap his feet inside his boots in plastic bags, make him wear gloves and mittens, walk with him to the bus stop, more to make sure that he stays bundled up than anything else. Marlys and I exchange waves and shouts of "Brr!" She and Paul, her husband, recently moved into town after twenty years' farming, so that he could indulge his real love, volunteer firefighting. The bedrooms are unbearable, so we drag our blankets into the living room and sleep near the stove with its masonry shell. There is no sun, so the insulated panels that we built to fit the windows are up all day. We are confined. Twice a day I shovel aside drifted snow and go out to the barn to feed the animals, muck out the goat pen, and milk the goats. We live like this at least once every year, and I haven't especially minded it in the past. Country people love to brag about the weather, to compare phenomenal details, like the cows' eyelids being frozen shut. Tom and I have a ritual when it gets cold like this—I run half a bucket of water, take it outside, and throw the water into the air. My grandfather swore that he had seen weather so cold that the water froze in glittering marbles before it hit the ground. I have never seen that, and I intend to in my lifetime if it is possible. Liz calls this my only ambition. Maybe. Tom is excited as soon as he wakes up each day—how cold is it? is it cold enough yet? is this the coldest place in the world? Bundles of sweaters and blankets and coats and pillows and socks pile up in the living room. After kerosene lamps day and night, the sojourns outside are blinding and huge, and it is hard not to be convinced that every exterior scene isn't somehow suspended in ice and time. We nap off and on all day, luxuriantly entwined with each other, stray items of clothing, the cats, layers of blankets. We read favorite bits of old books aloud but are too sleepy to stick with anything for long.

On Saturday, another bitter, overcast day, while I am breaking the ice in the goats' water bucket, I hear a car stop at the end of the lane, and not long after that Lydia Harris and a child, who must be Annabel, appear vividly on the path. They are carrying skates. Up in the house, I know,

Liz and Tom are rooting around in their blankets still, drinking parsley tea with honey and telling each other jokes. As I left, Tom was saying, "How many raspberries can you put in an empty bowl?" and Liz was pretending she didn't know. It seems to be fairly early morning, but in fact we let the clock wind down Thursday and forgot to set it yesterday by Tom's arrival home from school. It could be any time. The Harrises, gazing around rather hesitantly, make me keenly aware of the yellow hole in the snow off the side of the front porch, where Tom and I have been peeing. Liz, to whom I never even mentioned my invitation, hasn't been out of her nightgown since Wednesday.

Even so, they are a riveting picture, mother in jewel-green jacket and blue earmuffs, daughter in a parka so fuchsia-colored that it seems to expand as I look at it. The wind lifts a dry dusting of snow off the mounded drifts, and it whirls at their knees. Behind, the black filigree of the maple woods, snow on the mountains shading into snow in the clouds. It is the daughter who seems hesitant, from this distance almost sulky. She stops and Lydia pivots to talk to her, leaning down earnestly. Though I can hardly tell what she looks like, I can see a scowl on her face.

It's still there when I come up to them, and maybe that's the problem. She is a slender child, with a nutty complexion, a high, smooth forehead, and large eyes in wide-apart, flaring sockets. That she is a beauty in the making is a fact so present that talking around it is like not referring to a visible handicap. As I walk up to them, their conversation lingers in the dry, still air: "He said we should come when we felt like it. They don't have a telephone." "I'm embarrassed. I don't think it's nice to drop in." "Skating will be fun." Annabel throws me a hostile glance: my approach has robbed them of choice. She is not pleased, and it is obvious that hers is the pleasure most often consulted. Click click,

just like that, my dislike of the child is solid, in place, maybe
even permanent.

We walk slowly toward the house. Liz's face appears in
a window, disappears. I detour the Harrises through the
barn, show them the sheep and the goats, the cows, the
ponies, and the chickens. At the pony stall, Annabel Harris
snaps from sullen to eager. "The foal's a roan," she says.
"A strawberry roan with four white feet and a snip and a
star. I used to take riding lessons in Boston, before we
moved here." She throws her mother an angry glance. "My
favorite horse was a strawberry roan. His name was Billy."
It is the humble name of the horse, the way it makes me
see a tall, rib-sprung, hammer-headed old nag, that reminds
me she is a child. "I was in the canter class when we left."
I could allude to her riding the pony someday. It would
mean nothing, but I don't do it.

By the time we get to the house, Liz and Tom are dressed,
the blankets are folded and stacked, and water is boiling on
the woodstove. As we step in, stomping snow off our boots
and making a flurry, I call out, "Did I tell you the Harrises
might come and skate, Liz? I'm sure the pond is frozen all
the way to the bottom after this week. Tom, get your skates,
son. Time to get some fresh air." He stands in the middle
of the room, gawking at, perhaps, his nemesis.

Nevertheless, he wipes his nose, gets his skates from the
skate chest, finds his coat, and Liz, without saying a word,
does a surprising and impulsive thing. She steps up to Lydia
Harris and kisses her affectionately on the cheek, as if Lydia
knows and welcomes all the thoughts we have had about
her. And Lydia's response is intriguing—in the split second
between the knowledge that she is about to be kissed by a
virtual stranger, and the kiss, she grows a second, cooler
exterior, a skin separated from herself by a quarter-inch of
airspace, a storm-window skin. The kiss does not seem to

be followed by any discomfort, or even recognition, on Lydia's part. As for Liz, she glances at me, exhilarated by what she has done. "Yes! Go skating," she carols. "When you come in, I'll have some apricot buns. I've been longing for some apricot buns!"

The path to the pond is uneven and slippery. The buildings and beds, when we glance back at them, look humble and drab, poor rather than handmade, but the pond glitters invitingly where the wind has blown away the floury dry snow. Tommy's bragging to Annabel about how we swim in it all summer and skate on it all winter, and it's full of trout, too, seems the expression of my own thoughts. After all, function is the superior virtue, isn't it?

Annabel says, "I thought he said it was frozen to the bottom."

"We aren't going to fall through." Tom is a bit scornful.

"Well, where do the trout go? Are they frozen, too?"

"Of course not." He doesn't go on, nor does he turn to me for help. He says, "Can you skate?"

"I took lessons in Boston last winter."

In spite of lessons, the two children are about equal, and in fact have something of the same aggressive style. In no time at all, Annabel has shed her fuchsia coat (dropped it in the middle of the pond, and Lydia has fetched it and folded it neatly on a rock) and is racing Tom back and forth across the ice, two laps, then four, then six. She has as little glide as he does—their legs churn, their arms flail, but they never fall down. They shout at one another, at us, at nothing. Once Annabel simply peels off a scream. Lydia smiles, says, "Isn't that awful? I mean, it's only high spirits, but it's so piercing. Nathan's brother keeps saying he's going to get her a summer job as a screamer in horror movies."

"They have those?"

"Oh, sure. They don't want the actors to scream and strain their voices. Marcus says she has perfect natural technique—total relaxation of the vocal chords. I say, Don't encourage her. But she's always been a screamer."

Lydia is in no hurry to skate. She sits across from me on a large rock, looking around or watching Annabel. Every time her eyes come back to her daughter, her expression softens—the sculptured, dignified quality that is her natural demeanor grows momentarily receptive. It happens repeatedly, no matter what else she is doing or discussing. And when Annabel laughs, Lydia smiles. I have to admit that I sort of resent it, as if, in some peculiar way, Annabel were unworthy of such intensity.

"She's a pretty little girl."

"Oh, yes. And she knows it, too. I've been thinking lately that I made a mistake telling her all these years. My mama never let the word 'pretty' cross her lips, and when Annabel was a baby, she told me she was proud of that, proud of the way my sisters and I had so little vanity. But I knew that just because we never heard it didn't mean we didn't worry about it. My sister Zuby used to say that we must be awfully homely if even our mama wouldn't say we were pretty. So Annabel was, and I told her she was, and now she's very persnickety about what she wears and how her hair looks. I don't know. It must be different with boys."

And truly it must be, if Tom, as he is doing now, can wipe the snot off his nose with his glove, look at it, wipe it on his pants without a second thought for the bandana in his pocket.

"Well, actually, we don't even have a mirror in the house."

"Are you joking?"

"It isn't a moral statement of any kind, we've just never had one."

"How do you know what you look like when you go somewhere?"

"We look in a window, or we ask each other. Liz used

to say, before she would go to town, 'Well, do I look like a person who's going to be stopped and searched by the welfare department?' "

Lydia doesn't say anything. Will this be what offends her, finally?

I say, "I mean, for us, the point is to stay above a certain disreputable level, not to attain some fashion standard."

"My mama would love it." She smiles, this time at me rather than at Annabel.

I say, "Do you want to skate? Don't you think we should give these kids some competition? Besides, my ass is freezing."

"You go ahead. I'm not much of an athlete."

I stand up and shout, "Hey! Let's play tag! I'll be it!" I slither onto the ice, find my footing, and go at once for Tom, who is nearer. He almost evades me by stopping suddenly and turning, but I whip around and tag him. He goes for Annabel, then me, then Annabel again. When he touches her she screams, but leaps after him at once, almost catching him. I stand with my back to the pair of them, acting nonchalant. She chases him for a moment, then turns and tags me. Instantly I tag her back, as if we were evenly matched, and she glances up at me, not smiling, her face registering recognition of the antagonism between us. She skates after Tom, at first languidly, then quickly. He stumbles on a nick in the ice and she catches him and tags him. He tries to crawl away and they start laughing. They are children—the telling sign is that touching one another means nothing.

In the woods by the pond, hanging over an old maple stump, is the tractor-tire inner tube we use in the summer. It is partially deflated with the cold, but Tom grabs it and throws it across the ice, at Annabel. As it passes her, she sits in it and slides a foot or two, and then he is upon her, spinning her around and around. She staggers up and then wrests it away from him. He wipes his nose on his sleeve and churns after her. She pushes the inner tube across the pond, screaming. When he is just behind her, she swings it around and knocks him down with it. Lydia is on her feet at once, but Tom is up, laughing, chasing Annabel screaming across the pond. She is skating fast, her arms swinging. As she twists to look back at him, I see again how beautiful she is—broad shouldered, lithe, naturally strong—and I think, Catch her, catch her, wash her face with snow! I am as hostile and angry as I have been in years. He does not catch her, but she comes to the indistinct edge of the ice, and goes sprawling in the snow.

Once in a while, one is instantly punished. I am punished. She lies still. Under the snow could be rocks, jagged, unyielding. It is hard to remember. Tom is laughing and gasping. Lydia is still sitting down. That anger I felt a second ago is as lost to me, perhaps as fatal to her, as a stone loosed from a slingshot. There is another second, in which the breeze lifts Tommy's hat and carries it a yard or two across the ice, red on white. And then Lydia and I are kneeling in the snow at the edge of the pond and Annabel is pushing herself out of it with her arms. She is slow. Lydia, across from me, takes the child's face in her hands. She says, "Playing a little rough, sweetie pie?"

Annabel sobs.

Lydia lowers her voice, to get the girl's attention. "Does it hurt somewhere? Open your mouth."

She opens her mouth. There is blood around her teeth.

"Did you hit your teeth on something?"

Annabel sobs. Lydia turns her over, onto her lap. I begin feeling around the body print for stones.

"Annabel, talk to me."

"I bit my tongue."

"Did you hit your head on anything?"

"There don't seem to be any projecting stones."

Annabel shakes her head. "It's just my tongue. Don't let the blood get on my sweatshirt!" This last she cries out in a near panic. I pack together a handful of clean snow. "Put this in your mouth. That will stop the bleeding." She takes the snow, holds it politely in her hand.

"Put it in your mouth, sweetie," says Lydia. "He's right."

She cries, but she puts it in her mouth.

Fifteen minutes later, as we are climbing the path back to the house, we begin exchanging self-blame. I say, "I shouldn't have wound them up like that, playing tag." Lydia says, "I saw the edge of the pond coming. I should have shouted to her." I say, "I saw they were getting rough, and I should have said something." Lydia says, "I hate to be the kind of mother who's always saying be careful and watch out."

"What would your mama say?"

She laughs. " 'Any bones broken?' and 'Can she walk on it anyway?' "

I laugh.

"I shouldn't make a story out of Mama, but she's tough—right, Annabel?" Annabel nods, pacified but shaken. At the house, Liz has whole-wheat buns cooked upside down with dried apricots and maple sugar. Annabel won't even taste one.

5. 🐟 *February*

A few days later, it occurs to Liz and me simultaneously that Lydia and Annabel's visit only seems to have been routine, that we had better discuss it in light of the autumn's events, which now seem unpleasant but distant. The dread I felt, in particular, of a mysterious but inevitable disintegration, has proved groundless. Doesn't the Harrises' visit prove that some sort of assimilation has taken place? Didn't we demonstrate to Tom through our actions and our words that Lydia and Annabel were like any other friends or acquaintances, perfectly acceptable and welcome, different in no way? After Tom goes to bed, we sit by the stove and catalogue the signs:

"He wasn't any more shy, even at first, than he is with anyone else."

"He talked to her."

"He even tried to impress her. When we were walking down toward the pond, he was talking about fishing."

"He didn't get the look, either. That's what I was afraid of."

"He played rough with her, but she was up for it. And he didn't go overboard. When she fell, it sobered him right up, right there."

"That doesn't always happen."

"Their behavior was perfectly reciprocal. He didn't do anything inappropriate."

"And at the end he was quite polite to Lydia. I didn't detect any anxiety or fear of her, or revulsion. When she held out her hand, he simply took it."

"Well, I never thought he was a dyed-in-the-wool racist. I always thought he was just spouting something he'd heard." I pause, and Liz says, "I was worried for a while that he somehow got it from us."

"From your mother?"

Liz rolls her eyes. "He hasn't seen her since he was two. I'm sure when she was here the last time, she was far too busy deploring our living conditions to bother with his social education. I thought it might be genes or something." She looks over at the sound of my skeptical sniff and smiles. "Come on. We don't know every little thing we are communicating. We might think we weren't racist, but still let something drop."

"On what occasion? There were never black people in Moreton until now. We don't have television. We don't even have a radio or a record player."

"You know something? Annabel could be the first black person Tommy's ever seen, except in a magazine."

"I can't believe that." But we sit back and stare at one another, because suddenly our little boy's life, which we always think of as nestled into ours, even partaking, somehow, of what we did and saw before him, appears to us as it must to him, vast, whole. I say, "It is weird to think that this is all he's ever known."

Liz's glance is sly. "Wasn't that the point?"

I get up and adjust one of the window panels and take a turn around the room. It was, but when I think of it like this, it seems a little frightening. Liz calmly picks up her knitting, and though I am tempted to divulge my little flutter of panic, this sudden inner vacuum, still narrow as a hair, but real, I don't. I say, "Actually, I didn't find Annabel an especially attractive child."

"With those eyes? You must be blind!" Liz laughs.

"She has a very sour attitude." I know I sound harsh. "She thinks it's her right to be pleased with everything."

Liz eyes me.

"She just dropped her coat in the middle of the ice and expected Lydia to retrieve it."

Liz smiles.

"What?"

"Every time she said a word, you scowled. It's not our business."

"Most of her words were dissatisfied or unpleasant."

"She fell down and bit her tongue! She's seven years old, anyway."

"I'm glad she's not our kid."

"She's very pretty and graceful. And I bet she's smart, too, and I don't believe for a moment what the teacher said last fall about maybe she didn't understand the word 'nigger.' She doesn't have the easiest life."

"I would have thought the same thing if she were blonde and blue-eyed."

"I'm not accusing you of racism. Are we having a fight?"

"I think I'm having a fight with myself. But Tom was fine. He seemed perfectly accepting. I'd be surprised if the trouble weren't over now. They might even get to be friends."

I am agitated. I go out onto the porch to get some sticks of wood and look outward, and the sprays of stars washing through each other in the clear black sky above our valley fail to soothe me. That other constellation, the window lights of Moreton fanning across the flank of Snowy Top, seems to retreat rather than to open toward us; I am momentarily saddened, as if something has happened, but, of course, nothing has, and when I come in, Liz is sitting at her loom, a cup of tea steaming lazily at her side. Another cup is sitting by my chair, and the click of her shuttle and the rich sassafras fragrance seem like two halves of the same whole comfort, something I do not at the moment feel, though I can see it in the distance, moving toward me.

After two weeks in the barn, both the pony and the foal are frisky and rambunctious. The mare throws her head up as I lead her out the door, and flares her nostrils at the fresh scents. The foal trots forward a few steps, then halts, trembling, her furry ears flicking back and forth. She paws the crusty snow and snorts a ruffling, miniature snort. The mare neighs to her, and that seems to set her off. She races toward the pasture fence, bucking and kicking. Tom, sitting on the fence, laughs. "She feels good, doesn't she, Daddy? What a pretty girl! Come get the carrot. Here it is. Come get it." He waits. She stops a few feet from him, throws her head, and skitters away. The mare snorts and farts and shivers all the skin along her back, ambles into the snowy pasture. The foal sails in after, her brief tail pointing stiffly upward, like the tail of a deer. They might find something under the snow—it has melted down a few inches in the last two days, as we have had temperatures well above freezing, a Valentine's Day thaw.

The sky is clear. The air is mild and thick with sun-warmed rising moisture. The mountainsides close at hand are still white entangled with brown and tan, but the dark, brushy humps beyond are a deep, winy purple, reflecting the depths above them. I can see curve folding upon curve, no precipitous, spectacular summits, as out west, no glittering peaks blazing white above the tree line, but something more soothing, and more mysterious to me, the unending mansion of the forest, full of clearings, spaces, openings, cells, and each of these private rooms inhabited by some animal or insect or protozoan. We do not live in the easiest country—the ground is rocky and steep—but there is not a cubic inch that isn't rife with activity and the jostle of living competition. I have always found grandeur in this variety, and a ready vision of the Earth itself—if here, then everywhere, a rock molded into roundness by the eternal work of numberless paws, wings, feet, mandibles, roots, appetites, intentions.

It is Sunday, and Liz has not gone to church.

Tom's boots, which Liz got at the Goodwill before Christmas, are too big, so, when he goes out into the middle of the pasture, he lifts his feet and puts them down as if he were carrying something on his metatarsals. The coat we got was a lucky find: real goose and duck down, with a fur-trimmed hood. Liz sewed in a lining that she knitted to fit, wool, like a sweater, but covered with cotton so it wouldn't chafe. When he was a baby, she made him a suit out of sheepskin and wool. She cut a flat, baby shape out of a sheepskin, then sewed to it a crocheted top, wool on the outside, cotton on the inside. She could slip him into this in only a diaper and be confident that he was warm and comfortable. I built her a rocking bench with a turned spool barrier across part of the front, so that she could lay him next to her in his sheepskin pouch, then rock, coo, and have her hands free. I wonder what it would be like to raise a child with money. All his life we have been devising things for his benefit; he has been our experimental subject, and I admit he has been a good one, receptive, appreciative, flexible about ideas that looked good on paper but didn't work, like the knitted wool diaper covers that were supposed to wick moisture away from the baby so that it could evaporate. He is a good boy, and I love him, but lately I have been remembering Lydia Harris's face as she watched Annabel and then as she turned her over after her accident. There was an interest there that I wonder if I have ever felt, a spectator's interest that is not predicated on approval or disapproval. She liked to watch Annabel act. I like to see Tom act properly. At the time a cause and effect seemed to be at work—had she expected more of Annabel, Annabel would have behaved better. But now, even though I know that, I am envious of her pleasure, the way you get envious when some friend you think is years past romance falls in love again, gets to have a delicious rare liquor that you can't afford.

Right now Tom does act properly. He stands in the center of the pasture, relaxed and patient, waiting for the foal to come to him, to take the carrot and accept the halter. She paws the snow, snorts into it, rears up and bucks. He smiles, but he doesn't laugh. He knows he is the most intriguing object in the pasture, and that she is pointedly ignoring him. He holds out the carrot, and she does a funny thing—curls her upper lip back and tosses her muzzle rhythmically up and down six or seven times, then faces him, suddenly quiet. He holds out the carrot, but makes no other move. In the damp air, I can hear his low, encouraging chatter. Step by step she comes up to him. As she takes the carrot between her lips, he slips the halter up his arm and over her head. As soon as she finishes the carrot, he turns and leads her away. She follows, self-contained but docile. Liz says that cats and horses have an innate esthetic sense. Sometimes I agree. Tom and Sparkle march around the periphery of the pasture, developing good habits. He is all taken up by her.

Liz is standing between the barn and the root cellar, watching, not really presenting herself. Perhaps what she sees is an emblem of defeat to her, but I am relieved she is here, whatever her reason for staying home. There was never a time when I saw her leave that my eyes didn't follow her until she was out of sight, and that I didn't feel a gravelly stretching ache at the sight of her receding back. I like them contained here, where nothing is sudden or unknown. I wave cheerfully to my wife, and she waves cheerfully back. The foal flicks her ears but makes no unexpected moves. The mare, who has worked her way around the field, nuzzles in my jacket for her apple. I feed her with one hand and press the other up under her mane. Her winter coat is thick and coarse, warm and inviting. Rubbing the hard muscle in her crest is like giving my hand a delightful massage. She arches her neck and presses against my palm. Whether she has esthetic tastes or not, she certainly has sensual appetites. After twenty circuits of the pasture, Tom is ready to tie Sparkle to the fence and groom her. The mare follows them and nuzzles the foal two or three times, then resumes foraging in the thinning snow cover for the grass underneath.

The orchard has forty trees that I have planted—fifteen apples, five pears, five apricots, five peaches, five sour cherries, and five plums. The apricots, peaches, and plums I got when I did some work at a nursery in State College, and the sour cherries are an experimental variety that I grew for the university. The apples are all old varieties, and I got them all for free. It's an old hunter's tradition: to repay a farmer for being allowed to hunt on his land, you prune his overgrown orchard every so often. I also made a habit of picking up windfall apples, or digging up seedlings and bringing them back with me. Most of the orchards in these parts are a hundred years old, so the apple trees grow true to type, but the types are unusual, and I can only guess at what I have from asking older folks who visit and reading books in the library. They grow; we eat them and dry them and make them into sauce. A few trees that were bearing before the farmhouse burned down in the last century still produce every so often. Out of those trees I have pruned so much dead wood that they look Japanese, but I am de-

termined to save them. I love to prune. It is a perfect day
to prune: a day when spring is a certainty rather than a hope,
no matter how many more snowstorms we have to look
forward to.

While I am getting out my shears and saw, Tommy leads
the foal out of the pasture and back to the barn. She goes
quietly, and the mare follows. I look for the oil to lubricate
the joint of the pruning shears, and just after I find it, Tom
comes out of the barn, swinging the halter on his arm. I
say, "Did you make sure the latch was tight?" and he says,
"Yes, Daddy," and I promise myself to check. These moments are clear in my mind. I know these things are said.
Even though we have had this exchange a hundred times,
this time my instinct is to pay attention to it, and I do.

Plums and peaches and apricots, all you really need to do
is take off the dead wood, and make sure that sunlight can
get to the interior of the tree. Apples are more interesting,
and like to be given a shape. A well-pruned apple orchard
looks beautiful all year round, because, even when the leaves
have dropped, the limbs of the trees and the trees of the
orchard make a figure, crooked but graceful, ordered but
various. Liz calls the orchard my "stabile."

The pruning takes almost until dark, and the goats are
bleating to be fed and milked. By the time I come in, Tom
and Liz have already finished their potato soup and Tom,
worn out from climbing into the higher branches and setting
the saw for me, has gone straight to bed. I am tired, too,
and hungry for my own potato soup.

Liz sits with me. The soup is pungent and rich with mush-
rooms we picked and dried last spring, and I push my hunk
of dark bread into it, then eat the bread with my spoon.
The crust is chewy and delicious. Liz says, "We could breed
the pony again. Howard won't mind."

"It's such a big project."

"But we've done it once now. We know how to go about it. Tom is old enough to walk the pony over there, too. It's only a couple of miles."

"Ponies don't produce anything on a farm, they just eat."

"They produce great manure."

"Well, sheep manure is more—"

"They produce a sense of responsibility and ownership in the son."

I push my bowl across the table; Liz smiles and gets up to refill it. To her back, I say, "He is good with them. It won't be long before he gets beyond me, though. One pony, he can sort of play it by ear, especially this pony, because she's so even-tempered, but more than that, I don't know if we can handle it—"

"Howard can give us advice." She sets the bowl in front of me.

"Howard is full of advice, but I don't think he knows much, between you and me."

"I still think it's a good idea."

"I'll think about it."

"Can I say one more thing?"

"What?"

"He's had a hard year. He would love this."

"He made it hard for himself. I don't think we should reward him for that."

Her lips close tightly, disappear. She does not relinquish my gaze, though. It is probably better not to address these differences about the sources of his behavior. It is probably better to drop the subject, and I do. Fourteen years together have taught me the profound but laborious discipline of knowing when to press the point and when to stop. I cut another hunk of bread and lay it in the bowl. The thick soup seeps upward, and the bread inflates. Liz is a wonderful cook.

She leaves me at the table and goes over to her spinning wheel, which I built from a pattern in a magazine from the library. In the magazine it was constructed of pecan, but it looks better in black walnut, dark and silky. She sits on the stool and begins carding some of last fall's lamb's wool into airy little sausages, called "rolags," I believe. There is tension, but it is not about the pony. We always have projects that we raise and discuss and disagree on. What is unspoken of is the church issue, and the time to discuss it is approaching. All day, though she has been calm and smiling and even jovial from time to time, I have imagined her tight and angry. I know this is guilt talking. I have imagined myself, too, those fifty-five or sixty Sundays, never failing to undermine her—asking her where she is going when I know, suggesting something complicated and delicious for breakfast in front of Tom so that she will have to disappoint him (I did that three times), making something complicated and delicious for breakfast that she would have to miss (I only did that once), receiving her good-bye kiss stiffly, as if insulted, telling her over and over that she didn't have to apologize or ask permission to go, never giving her an opening so that she might ask me to attend some function with her, never making it easy for Tom to go along. But she has persevered in attendance, participation, prayer. She has carried home funny bits and entertained me with them, she has spoken naturally and fondly of people I haven't met. She has, in fact, been rather a holy person, virtuous and patient.

This morning she just stayed home. I asked her if she was feeling ill. She wasn't. We had oatmeal and dried peaches for breakfast. The dishes were cleaned up in plenty of time. But then, instead of putting on her coat, she sat down at her knitting, a sweater for herself. I went outside. I kept my eye on the door, but it never opened until she called us in for lunch. Now, eight or ten rolags ranged beside her, she starts to spin. She pushes the treadle with her foot, and the large wheel begins to turn the bobbin with a clicking whir. Her fingers work precisely, and the spindle draws the thread from them, twisting the fibers of wool together into a kind of flowing, almost liquid line. She says, "Are you going to do something or just watch me?"

"We should have walked in to the library yesterday. It wasn't that cold."

"You haven't read that last book. I thought you wanted to read that."

"I could do some washing."

"Do you really want to start that? It's nearly nine-thirty."

I feel balked, restless. Maybe she isn't going to bring it up after all. The clicking whir continues through our conversation. The house seems cramped. I go to the window and look toward Moreton, trying to make out Lydia Harris's mullioned windows. I imagine each pane alight, the chandelier tinily reproduced twenty or forty times, Lydia in some vivid blue, reading in a bright chair, music playing.

"Are you upset, Robert?"

"Do I seem upset?"

"You've seemed sort of edgy all day."

"Is that angry edgy or anxious edgy?"

"Why don't you tell me?"

"I was hoping you would make the diagnosis. I'm not sure. Why didn't you go to church?"

She laughs a full, merry laugh. "It isn't church."

"Your Fellowship Meeting."

"I didn't feel like it." She laughs again.

"Why are you laughing? You've been very serious about this for more than a year."

"I can't do it anymore. It's too strenuous."

"The walk?"

"It's more like a trudge upstream."

"We walk to town all the time."

"Yes, WE do. It's not the walk, it's the departure. The whole trip is one long departure from you and Tom and the place and the routine."

"I knew you were thinking that. I was trying to make you think that. I wanted it to be hard for you."

"Well, that part was fun, actually."

"It was?"

"That you wanted it to be hard? Of course. It gave me just the little push I needed to get going, or to get out of bed in the cold and say my prayers."

I must look a little shocked, because she regards me for a long minute, without smiling, but with a ready, receptive look on her face, as if she is taking me in anew. She says, "Bobby, you know that the urge for revenge is a fact of marital life." And then, "You always think too well of me. I love you partly because you never fail to see beauty in what you look at, but that scares me, too."

"I see beauty in you."

"Don't evade me!" Her eyes snap and she is suddenly angry. "There is something about each other that each of us has to see! If you come too close, it will go out of focus, and we won't see it."

"What is it?"

"I don't know. I'm working that out. I've been working that out all day."

I have to say that I don't know what she is talking about, or even how to understand what she is getting at. It shouldn't surprise me that this churchgoing loops into our marriage, but it frightens me a little bit, as if she could now quit anything, having quit that. I close my mouth and go outside to take a leak off the porch. I can tell a lot of snow has melted by how the hole we made has sunk through to brown grassy earth. I cast my eyes around the place, toward the barn. No noises, no disturbances. No reason there should be. When I go inside, the argument has already begun.

"Why do you just walk away?"

"I had to piss."

"You had to evade this issue."

"What issue?"

"I can't believe you. I simply can't."

We don't often argue this way, mired in our different modes of perception, and when we do I think it is because we don't know what we are arguing about, or, if she does, I don't. I cling to this one fact, that she didn't go to her meeting today. I say, "I don't know why we are angry. I don't know what we are arguing about."

"You are simply indifferent to the fact that I've been wrestling with one of the central issues of our lives! You walk away from me as soon as I bring it up!"

"Bring what up? You haven't brought anything up!" I realize that I am entering into the absurdity of all of this, but the thing about absurdity is that it isn't only funny, it is also disorienting and grating.

"I am trying to bring it up. I am literally trying to bring something up, as if I were choking on it, but I don't know what it is! Why don't you help me?" And she bursts into tears.

There must be an appropriate response to this, not an action but a feeling or an understanding that something is at stake, that something is lost or about to be. There must be a sadness here that I could enter into, like a closet, but the quickness of her reactions—we can't have begun this conversation more than fifteen minutes ago, and she has laughed, smiled, listened, gotten angry, wept—blasts all reaction out of me. I stand carefully, as if the house had settled badly. I begin very slowly. I say, "How is it bad that I see beauty in you?"

"It's untrue."

"I truly see beauty in you."

"It's just a mistake. I can't explain it." She sits on the floor cross-legged, tears finished, exuding an air of devastation that will soon eddy into every corner and wash back through our history together. This is not the first time, but these are rare and delicate moments, moments when the seeking, probing quality of her inner life demands something of me that I don't understand and can't give, but also when the life I had thought of as a solid is suddenly lit from within, hollow and fragile, tempting me to break it for revenge. I do understand that; yes I do.

Liz is right that my responses are primitive ones, mostly sensuous. Many days pass in which I simply make my way through the hours, make my way around the place. Much of my mental time is spent registering impressions, and when Liz and I remember things, I always remember that there was a strong odor of snake or that the ground was soft or that the trout had coriander leaves sprinkled over it. It must be that I have a strong esthetic sense, since I recognize right and wrong juxtapositions of shapes, tastes, colors, textures continually, like some kind of clocking mechanism that is never turned off. I recognize them, often rearrange them, but I don't inquire into them. Mostly I hate this argument because it is esthetically jarring, and because a part of me that is undeveloped is being called upon to respond appropriately. "That's enough now," is what my grandfather would have said. The most I dare is a dramatic, annoyed sigh.

Liz looks at me for a long moment, then heaves herself up, wipes the hair out of her face, and goes into the kitchen. I move to the table, and start leafing through one of the library books stacked there, *Complete Berries and Tree Fruits*. The fact is, I betray her almost at once by sinking into the text, slipping out of the argument as out of a husk.

At bedtime she says, mildly, "You've forgotten about everything we said, haven't you?"

"No." I step out of my overalls, and decide to come clean. "I have sort of absented myself from it, though."

"You will never change."

No answer for that one.

In bed, in the dark, she says, "There wasn't room in my life for two of you."

"Two of me?" My tone is light, but I am thinking, suddenly and irrationally, that it is a lover she has been going to see, driving in his car with him, his convertible. I speak bravely. "Two of us?"

"There isn't any other man."

I inhale again. I used to smoke in the army, and this would be a good time for a cigarette.

"You and God." She settles herself for sleep. Her words have a bubblelike quality in the dark, self-contained and enigmatic. I have no sense that I have understood anything since I put away the pruning tools.

I awaken and dress in this state of confusion, very early, before dawn, and it deepens as soon as I step off the porch and catch sight of the barn in the half light. The barn door is ajar, and the mushy snow is muddied with many hoofprints. I follow two sets, pony and foal, as they meander away from the barn, toward the paddock, then away, toward the pond. I think that I will see them from the top of the rise, but I don't, and begin to run. The ground is wet and slippery. I fall a couple of times, which disorients me more. Over and over, I wonder what time it is.

The pony mare is hidden in the woods on the far side of the pond. She is simply standing in the uncommunicative way equines have, looking at the pond. I turn and survey the pond once, twice. The foal is nowhere, though I note that the ice by the intake has melted, and water is flowing freely and fast out of the stream that feeds the pond. I check the pony. Her legs are wet and cold. She has been in the pond. I look at the pond again; then I see the strangest thing that I have ever seen—the dark form of the foal, stretched out and shadowy under the ice, unmoving. I step toward it. The ice is thick enough to hold me, but clear enough to make out the foal's white markings. I stand over it. The mare looks at me steadily, and I see in her gaze not indifference, but animal endurance. I squat down on the ice and lay my hand over the foal, and I cannot help weeping.

Sometime later, when I am leading the mare away from her position in the woods (she is balky and reluctant, and I am trying to be kind to her), Tom appears at the top of the rise. He shouts, "Hey, Dad—," but then he stops and stares, taking everything in, asking no questions. The mare slows me down. When he turns and runs away, I can't follow him.

At the breakfast table, he is eating steadily. He gives me a covert glance when I slam through the door; Liz is on me at once—where's the foal, has something happened to the foal? Tom watches, his eyes flipping back and forth between us, as we hash it out, the night-time escape, their progress toward the pond, how maybe they were trying to get a drink, or the filly was simply frolicking near the intake, the ice broke, the current was fast and the bottom slippery, an accident, very unusual, even for the ponies to go out on the ice. We talk furiously for a while, then sigh, fall silent. Liz cries. I say, "The mare is fine. We can breed the mare again—" It is late. Tom hears the school bus and jumps from the table. We stuff him into his things, and he runs for the end of the lane. The school bus waits and, after a long while, I hear it gear up as it pulls away. Marlys Tillary knows our clock situation. It occurs to me later that I could have let him stay home.

After the morning chores (the mare is whinnying and

kicking in her stall), Liz and I take ropes and an ax down to the pond and chop a hole in the ice. It is immediately apparent that though the ice over the foal is about two inches thick, the whole pond is unstable. We work quickly, splashing, wetting ourselves, soon shaking with cold. The foal comes up headfirst, frozen stiff, and now that we have her, it isn't clear what we are going to do with her. Normally we would bury her in the woods, but the ground is frozen. Howard, of course, would suggest the dead animal removers—pet food. We leave her in the woods near the pond and go into the house to dry off and warm up.

It is hard for a farmer not to take a practical attitude toward animal death. Cats, for example, roam our place, and do a good job keeping the mice down. We pet the cats, and give them names, and admire the variety of their personalities, but we don't feed them, and we are used to their hunting techniques as well as their population management practices. I have seen litters born in the winter disappear within two days—the mother eating her young simply because it is too cold for them to survive. I used to trade for a hog and a beef steer every year, name them, raise them, slaughter them, eat them. I fish for trout all season, and I hunt, too. But the fact is, I've let the last few years go by without bothering to get a beef calf or a shoat or a venison. I don't keep a milk cow anymore, and I haven't shot a duck or a Canada goose since Tommy was a baby. We don't often slaughter a chicken. It is not a moral position, but it is a disinclination to undergo too many animal deaths. I have to say that I regret this softness in myself, because the world we have here is less fertile and lively because of it— presents fewer experiences, fewer relationships, fewer moral problems. I think it is good to experience one's power over the animal, to treat it well, house it properly, give it a good life and a painless death, to feel with one's own hands the bloody cost of one's appetites, and to know viscerally what one is like—one is like an animal, one lives in nature, where death is.

Even so, the death of the foal is shocking and important. Liz cries again. Over lunch we can't help reminiscing about how cute she was, what a pretty pony she was turning into, how good Tom was with her. The overcast day is ugly to us, its slop no longer a harbinger of spring, but a menacing eternity of discomfort. When Tom comes home, he has had a bad day—Miss Bussman got on him twice for not paying attention, and he dropped his math book in a mud puddle as he was getting on the bus, and two children stepped on it before he could get off the bus and pick it up. He doesn't talk about the foal, but he sniffles at the table while eating his snack and whines that we should have a television, though he knows not only that there is no electricity, but in these mountains there is minimal TV reception.

"Annabel Harris got a satellite dish. They get a hundred and thirty-seven channels."

"That's a hundred and thirty-seven chances to get stupid. We'll go to the library on Saturday."

The look washes over him like water from a bucket. He stands up suddenly, knocking his chair over, tipping his milk. He shouts, "I hate reading. That's what's stupid, those books!"

Liz is soothing, "You'll get better at it. You get better every day. The teacher says you're really doing well."

"I don't care! I don't want to!"

I must inhale sharply, because Liz throws me a flattening glance, so I keep my mouth shut. Tommy storms upstairs. That's the first day.

By noon of day two, ours is a universe of snow. Low-hanging clouds seal in our valley, and the blizzard floats in the quiet air, accumulating on tree limbs and roofs inch by inch, but offering no threat. My grandfather would have called this a "corn snow," and told me that in a few days all of this would sink right into the soil, good moisture for this summer's crops to draw upon, a gift of practical benefit as well as of beauty. A gift, too, for Liz and me, of suspended time, a universe of silent white noise, lulling us into a nap sometime after lunch. The house is warm, though the windows are uncovered, and it is exhilarating, like skinny-dipping, to strip in the living room, to be free of overalls and long underwear and modesty, to feel the touch of my own hands on my skin, as well as to anticipate hers.

The snow seems to give the minutes a marvelous, languid lag. We are taking our clothes off at a quarter to one, and I notice that it is almost one-thirty as I am dozing off. The nap is one of those snoozy, hypnotic ones, half awake but entirely relaxed, with no dreams, only the contented awareness of cottony white light, minute after easy minute. At two-fifteen I turn over, and think that we have more than an hour to ourselves before the bus comes. Liz, her hip pressed into my thighs, her braid unraveled across the pillow, curls her toes in her sleep and hooks a foot around my ankle. When I awaken again, it is, miraculously, still two-fifteen. I stretch. The room is beginning to cool, which means that the fire needs wood. It is only when I get up to feed it that I realize that the wonderful luxury of time has only been a function of my sleepy state of mind. In fact, the gloom of late afternoon is beginning to take hold, though admittedly earlier than usual because of the overcast. The clock has stopped.

I am slow. It is hard to tell what time it is with this weather, and the utter relaxation of my nap still grips me. I throw some wood on the fire, pausing to stare thoughtlessly at the glowing coals. Liz groans and sighs, throws out an arm. Her eyes still closed, she says, "What time is it? Was that the bus? God, I feel lazy."

The snow has slacked off. When I step to the window, I

see that the cloud cover has lifted off the valley. My guess is it will be clear tomorrow.

"Where's Tommy?" She is sitting up straight. "It's going to be dark soon."

The sudden wedge of panic leaves me breathless. All at once we are groping for socks and overalls and boots, but I have no thoughts, unlike Liz, who realizes that he must have come in, seen us asleep, and headed for the woods behind the pond, intending to investigate the pony foal. She runs there while I check his room, the barn, and the workshop. We call, but it is frustrating in the muffling snow. Truly it is late. The goats are bleating in the barn to be milked and fed. By the time I join her at the pond, it is real twilight. The snow around the mound of the foal is undisturbed, as is the surface of the pond. He is nowhere near here. And now our faculties click in. The page of snow is revealing. It reveals that no child's boots have made a path of any sort from the head of the lane, that Tom is nowhere on the place.

More faculties click in. We make a plan—I will ski to town and make some calls, after checking at the school. She will wait here and do the milking. If he can't be found, I'll get Martin Summerbee to drive me around, and I will also call the police. The plan forestalls panic. I stand on the porch tying my tassels and then locking on my skis. I shake the right ski. It holds. I shake the left. The door slams as Liz goes inside for the milking basin. As I stand up from readjusting my gaiter over my boot, I see the sinuous, living yellow light of a huge fire down the valley, and I know at once that it is Lydia Harris's house, and that this is the last time I will ever look outward and see it beckon.

I ski directly for it. The snow is fluffy and light on top, damp and slushy underneath, not the best skiing snow. Rabbits, deer, and pheasant flee my approach. More than once, I have to stop and wipe the ice off my eyelids and mustache. At the bottom of my land, it takes me a while to get through the barbed wire in the dark, then to make my way over the running creek at the bottom of my neighbor's land. Moreton isn't far, and it is a big blaze. I do not lose sight of it. It shifts its shape—boxy first, tall and wide as the house, then low, then suddenly tall and narrow. When I stop shushing my skis, I can hear windows pop. There is no yelling or screaming. I would have expected yelling and screaming. The Moreton Volunteer Fire Department plays lights upon it as well as hoses. Even after the hoses are quiet, the lights continue to scan the blackened framework. Then I come to the bottom of the wooded hill below the house, and the whole scene is hidden from view. I take off my skis and clamber across that brook, then push through the new snow, up the steep hill. It is tiring work, this cross-country trek from my place to Lydia's, harder than I had thought it would be. What is my state of mind? Suspended. Expectant. Annoyed at the effort. I haven't as yet considered Lydia or Annabel. When I crest the hill, the first thing I see in the scanning light is the arch of the satellite dish beside the garage. The second thing I see is Paul Tillary, the chief of the volunteer fire department. His hands are gripping the shoulders of Tom Miller, my son, and he is speaking to him in deadly earnest.

6. 🍂 November

The fact is, though there have been police and welfare investigators and lawyers and fire investigators and tax assessors and real-estate and insurance people and perhaps other nameless officials as well, the first time I see Lydia Harris after the fire isn't until a few days past Halloween. I am on a bus in State College, heading for work. It stops for a light as the door to a pleasant brick house opens. It is a long light, so I can watch Lydia check that the door is locked, secure the strap of her bag over her shoulder, and descend the front steps. She is wearing a red coat, long and generously cut, with blue high heels. At the curb, she crosses with the light that is against us; then the light changes and I lose sight of her.

Tom, on the other hand, has seen Annabel twice, though they go to different schools. At the end of the summer he saw her inside an ice cream parlor he was passing, and in September she performed in a citywide talent show that gave assemblies at each grammar school. She played a clarinet solo.

At the university, I set concrete forms for the new biotechnology center. I make twelve dollars an hour, and the job will last through the winter. In the spring, the foreman says, they will put me on interior carpentry. Though the building will be concrete from top to bottom, they have decided to include woodwork—floorboards, window trim, benches in alcoves. Liz works in the university bookstore as a clerk. She makes six-fifty an hour, and since she works for the state, she has good benefits. When we first moved into State College, she worked as a waitress at a very nice restaurant, and sometimes brought home a hundred dollars in a night, but she didn't like the work. Tom has a paper route. We have found it hard, at times, to keep busy enough. Tom sees a counselor three times a week, we see her once a week. The state welfare department pays half the cost. The terms of our continued custody of our son demand that he pursue the counseling until the counselor dismisses him, and that he be gainfully and regularly employed. The children at his new school may or may not know about the Harrises' house. The teacher, Miss Donohue, does, as does the principal, Mrs. Griffin, and the school counselor, Mr. Searls.

We have reconstructed Tommy's actions of that afternoon. The key, in my view, was that school was called off for the afternoon, on account of snow conditions. When Marlys Tillary asked where Tom was, Sam MacDonald, a third-grader, volunteered that Tom was skiing home with me, which was what Tom had told him. Tom had no trouble finding the Harrises' house, having heard Liz and me discuss exactly where on Laurel Creek Road it was. The walk, in the whirling but peaceful snow, took him about forty-five minutes. Lydia was still in State College, and Annabel had gone to her regular after-school care-giver. Tom had plenty of time, and he looked things over pretty carefully, including the satellite dish, Annabel's playhouse, the sleds and cross-country skis leaning against the back porch, the open garage. He tried the doorknobs, but the doors were locked. The storm windows prevented that sort of entry. I think at this point he was in an investigative mood, maybe nothing more. He went back to the garage a second time, and that's when he found the kerosene the Harrises kept for heating the upstairs on especially cold days. He was perfectly familiar with kerosene. He took it out to the satellite dish and began pouring it at the base of the stand, then, spying the cable from the dish to the house and hoping, somehow, to set fire to the TV, he poured kerosene all along the cable to where it entered the house beside the back porch. He carried the can up onto the porch, where he stumbled in his too-large boots and spilled the kerosene over the porch floor. It dripped over the edge onto the latticework around the foundation of the porch. He left the can on the porch.

There were also safety matches in the garage, for lighting the workshop heater. Tom returned to the garage and took them from their spot on the shelf (neatly labeled "matches"). He lit the satellite dish. The state arson investigator counted this out for me. "Ten feet of cable?" he said. "Twelve? One banana two banana three banana four banana five banana six banana it's on the porch. By ten banana, with all that kerosene, it's established in the siding and moving into the eaves. Once it gets into the attic, then the house is fully involved."

A car inches along Laurel Creek Road, the driver peering into the blizzard. His ventilation system carries to him the smell of burning. He checks his gauges. His engine is not overheating. He ignores it, then looks in the rearview mirror. Black smoke is pouring upward from Lydia Harris's house. Flames can be seen, shooting from the roof. A little boy is standing at the edge of the yard, just where the creek flows under the road, his hands in his pockets. Seven minutes later, when the Moreton volunteers arrive on the scene, there isn't much they can do.

When I expressed surprise at the speed of events, the fire investigator laughed. He said, "Every house-fire has the same potential. Not every one achieves it, but a wooden residential structure can become fully involved within ten minutes." He also said, "I'm not saying it happens every day, but with juvenile arson you've got to look at the envy factor."

I said, "Juvenile?"

He said, "Little boys. If it were a girl, you'd have something really to worry about."

The school counselor, Mr. Searls, said, "Now, who was more different from the others than Tom? A little black child, that's who. I'm not surprised."

We have a two-bedroom apartment. The kitchen is fairly large, and the landlord has given me permission to set up my workshop in the basement, but I haven't had, or made, the chance.

Insurance and real-estate people decided in the spring that our place was worth over seventy-five thousand dollars, especially since the barn was in such good repair. The Harris house, including all the furnishings, clothing, computer hardware and software, and sundry other equipment, was worth $140,000, replacement cost. Her insurance company is suing me to recover some of their loss. They are making their case on the basis that Liz and I knowingly lived in a negligent way, that, had we owned a telephone, more than one clock, a car, we could have had our son under greater control and prevented the arson. My lawyer says that the case is not as clear-cut as the insurance company makes it out to be. He is intrigued. We will talk about the fee later, he says. I suppose that a precedent could be set that might refer only to me, since I am the only person anyone knows who lives this way. Or lived this way.

We have a telephone, three clocks, and, as of a week ago, a car, a 1983 Dodge Colt, one owner, forty-seven thousand miles.

I would be happy to give them the place, but my lawyer

and my counselor are against it. The lawyer says that, the way State College is growing, I could get much more for it in a few years, not to mention the fact that the insurance company should not be allowed to bully me; the counselor says that I should make no life-changing decisions during the first year of counseling.

We have a television. When we were arguing about buying it, Liz took a moral stand against trying to live separately from the general culture. In the heat of anger, she called me a "megalomaniac." Later she apologized and took it back.

On the day we bought the car, Tina's book arrived in the mail, forwarded from Moreton. The chapter about me was one of the shorter ones, and though she didn't call me a genius there, she did say, in the introduction, "and Bob Miller shows what must be a variety of genius in the single-minded way he has transformed his valley, and his life, to an expression of ideals that are often extolled, but almost never realized." Liz read the chapter and wept. The next day she took the book to our counseling session (we drove), and it came out that she was angry with me for not weeping, for reading with greater interest the much longer chapter on prehistoric varieties of corn. The counselor reiterated her view that I have not participated in the grieving process, and said that, while Liz's anger wasn't entirely justified, since we all own our own feelings, it was understandable. I took the book in my hands again, leafed through the chapter, looking for what has been lost. I wished there had been pictures.

I haven't wept since a few days after the fire, before we even knew what would happen to us. I was standing in the barn, currying the pony, and I knew that I had reached the utter empty-handed end of knowledge about how to raise this child. I dropped the curry comb and walked to the barn door, where I looked at the house and the winter-ravaged beds facing it, and all my habits of thought presented them-

A NOTE ON THE TYPE

The text of this book was set in a digitized
version of Bembo, a well-known Monotype face.
Named for Pietro Bembo, the celebrated
Renaissance writer and humanist scholar who was
made a cardinal and served as secretary to
Pope Leo X, the original cutting of Bembo was
made by Francesco Griffo of Bologna only a few
years after Columbus discovered America.
Sturdy, well-balanced, and finely proportioned,
Bembo is a face of rare beauty, extremely
legible in all of its sizes.

Composed by Crane Typesetting Service, Inc.,
Barnstable, Massachusetts

Printed and bound by Fairfield Graphics,
Fairfield, Pennsylvania

Designed by Mia Vander Els

let Tom's innocence lie next to his envious fury; let Liz's grief for the farm lie next to her blossoming in town; let my urge to govern and supply every element of my son's being lie next to our tenuous custody; let the poverty the welfare department sees lie next to the wealth I know was mine. If these things are allowed, if no wholes are made, then it seems to me that I can live in town well enough, and still, from time to time, close my eyes and feel a warm, wet breeze move up the valley, hear the jostling and lowing animals in the barn, smell the mixed scent of chamomile and wild roses and warm grassy manure, and remember the vast, inhuman peace of the stars pouring across the night sky above the valley, as well as the smaller, nearer, but not too near, human peace of the lights of Moreton scattered over the face of Snowy Top.

They have quickly filled him in on who's who in the super-hero universe, and he is saving part of his newspaper money for a hipper bicycle, one with solid metal spoke covers.

Liz, too, is more naturally attuned to this life, though she has cried and suffered over the change, over our loss and shame, over my present "aimlessness." Still, she eats lunch with friends she has made at work, and also does something I remember my mother doing—traveling around the kitchen, sink to stove to refrigerator, telephone receiver wedged between cheek and shoulder. We have a bathtub. She spends a lot of time there. She goes to the Episcopalian church.

As for me, I think often of Lydia Harris, her dignity, her slender but muscular hands, the very African shape of her head, the grace that she never failed to express. I think of her, and Annabel, too, with what seems like love. Once in a while, I think that if I could talk long enough and eloquently enough, I could make Lydia understand, but I don't know what I would have her understand, and events have carried us beyond communication, anyway. For a long time, I looked for some kind of judgment at her hands. Now I can imagine what it would be, and anything I might say would sound, at least to me, like excuses.

Liz and the counselor have a program mapped out aimed at "recovery." One of the counselor's handouts pictures this as a ladder, with a man climbing steps labeled "denial," "anger," "bargaining," and so forth. I am loitering at the bottom of the ladder, I suppose. But it seems to me that what they want of me is to make another whole thing, the way I made a whole of my family, my farm, my time, a bubble, a work of art, a whole expression of my whole self. No, I say, though only to myself (the counselor has real power over our custody arrangement). Let us have fragments, I say. Let the racial hatred that has been expressed through us lie next to the longing I feel for Lydia Harris;

selves simply as varieties of pride. Even the love I had been so sure of—for Tommy and Liz, for the valley, for this work, this soil, this air—was primarily self-inflating. I stood paralyzed at the doorway, blinded by tears. That was the only time.

It is without question too soon for the truth. In the meantime, it will be nineteen years in May since I got out of the army, since I bought the land. That June, while I was gathering materials to build the house, I lived in a tent down by the pond. I cooked over a fire that I built on a flat rock. Mostly I grilled trout and drank water. I walked into town for supplies, and one day I bought a trowel and a five-pound bag of mortar. The next day I built a little fireplace out of stones. I laid the stones and mortar over an old cardboard box, and into the top, what would become the floor of the fire compartment, I set thick sticks in a grid, about two inches apart. When the mortar had set but not hardened, I pulled the sticks out, carefully, leaving ventilation holes for the fire. Then I peeled the box away. I built ten-inch walls around the fire floor, and that night walked back into Moreton and strolled the alleys. I knew I would find an old grill in someone's trash, and I did, perfect size and shape, exactly what I had imagined. I was not surprised.

When I look back on the succeeding eighteen years, I see someone, neither boy nor man but a nameless intermediate form, who has received as a gift an endless number of wishes. The only rule governing these wishes is that they must be specific. And of course they are, because particularity is his genius (inclination, prevailing spirit). But the moral of all wish tales is that, though wishes express power or desire, their purpose is to reveal ignorance: the more fulfilled wishes, the more realized ignorance.

Tom likes it in town. He has a group of friends on our block and the next one, four boys who ride bikes, read comic books, play endless wavelike games of territorial defense.